First published in Great Britain in 2018 by
HOT KEY BOOKS
80–81 Wimpole St, London W1G 9RE
www.hotkeybooks.com

A CIP catalogue record for this book is available from the British Library.

ISBN: 9781471407116
also available as an ebook

2

This book is typeset using Atomik ePublisher
Printed and bound by Clays Ltd, Elcograf S.p.A

Hot Key Books is an imprint of Bonnier Zaffre Ltd,
a Bonnier Publishing company
www.bonnierpublishing.com

CHLOE COLES

BOOKSHOP

GIRL

HOT
KEY
BOOKS

Note from Chloe

I have spent a huge four-finger-Kit-Kat-sized chunk of my life in bookshops. I've grown up in them really. I got my first ever bookselling job at the tender age of sixteen, when I still had braces and flat hair and pretended to know about some c'mon-everybody's-read-it classic or broke out in a cold sweat every time I fumbled around on a keyboard looking up authors I'd never heard of.

Since then, so much has happened. I've made best friends for life and fallen in love and had my heart broken and my braces ripped off. I've opened exam results and moved cities and found new bookshops and fallen in love again and worked out that Minstrels are probably my fave snack to scoff behind the till. I've graduated and met my childhood heroes and fangirled myself to tears and I have imagined, time and time again, what it would be like to see my very own book on one of the shelves. So I decided to write something.

Something about a teenage girl working in a bookshop. Something about finding your voice and your people.

I hope you enjoy it. (And if you don't, well, just make sure you don't damage the spine. Booksellers never refund a damaged spine.)

Chloe x

PIGEON TITS

I'm running late.

Not that I'm actually *running*. I don't think I've ever run in my entire life. Thank *God* I'll get to drop PE next year. I reckon I've spent most of my education hatching plans to get out of cross-country or swimming. I even claimed to have asthma in Year Six so the teachers would get off my back for 'not trying'. It was believable enough; the asthmatic girls always outran me anyway.

So, okay, I'm not running, but I *am* in a hurry.

Today is officially my day off work, and it has so far consisted of about twelve slices of toast, a box of Jaffa Cakes, one and a half documentaries on Netflix and a gazillion repeats of *The Shangri-La's Greatest Hits*, which inspired two hours of hair and make-up 'experiments'. Unfortunately Tony, my boss, called me mid-fringe trim.

I had him on speaker phone while I concentrated on my 'do, and agreed to trek into work for some announcement or training or something . . . I just couldn't seem to get my fringe even and kept snipping away. Now it looks less Bettie Page and more like a nit-recovery hair-hack.

Here I am, sweating my way up the hill towards town, the evidence of the Great Fringe Assassination sticking to my forehead already. Holly's house is on the way; I text her to say I'm a lot nearer than I really am. She'll know I'm late. I'm the one who's always late. She's the one who can fit a McDonald's straw in the gap between her two front teeth.

Greysworth town centre on a summer's afternoon. The *sights*. Everywhere I look I see flipflops smacking onto swollen, cracked heels as they tread past empty shop units. Lads on bikes, riding with no hands and no shirts as they suckle on sports bottles, looking like big, bald babies. I pass a man urinating against the window of M&S. It's slightly uphill so the pee trickles back down towards him and over his shoes.

I'm trudging along the main road in the blistering heat when all of a sudden I hear, 'OI-OIIII!!! NICE ARSE!!!!'

A white van hurtles past with two rowdy lads inside. The bloke in the passenger seat pokes his head out of the window with his tongue flapping out of his mouth. He looks like an actual dog. I feel my cheeks burn with embarrassment.

Since I started working at Bennett's Bookshop two months ago, I've made an attempt to read my way through the entire Women's Studies section and, believe me, I've read enough by now to know that men shouting things about my body as I mind my own business is *not* a compliment; it's actually street harassment.

Nice arse. They have no idea.

It makes my menstrual blood *boil* to be spoken to like that.

I'm still seething when I see Holly.

'Hi, Hols. Would you rather suffocate a sexist creep to death with pickled-onion crisp packets or fling a used tampon through the window of his white van of misogyny?'

'*Who?* What are you talking about?'

I relay the sorry tale to my bestie as she rolls her eyes and links her arm in mine.

She groans. 'What *is* it with blokes thinking they can do that? It's so boring. So unoriginal. Don't they know that we've heard it all before? *I* spent the whole of Year Six being referred to as "Pigeon Tits" by that idiot Charlie Jones and his mates! *Remember?!*'

'I do remember.' Throwback to what a pain in the ovaries *he* was. 'I remember him singing "Come Fly With Me" at you as he rubbed his nipples through his sweatshirt. Shame that level of creativity seems to be lost on the white-van men of this town.'

She shakes her head with disgust. 'Crisps are far too good for that *nice-arse* loser, *especially* pickled onion! Soggy tampon for him. Easy.'

As I smile, I notice Holly's eyes move up towards my forehead. 'It looks so, so bad, doesn't it?!' I cringe, trying to smooth the hair down with my fingers, like this will somehow magic back some length.

'*No*, it's just a lot shorter than usual . . .'

'I blame whatever's going on at Bennett's. Tony interrupted my snipping session.'

'He sounded so stressed out when he called, didn't he?'

I laugh. Tony is always stressed. 'Pffft, what's *new*, pussycat?'

CASUALTY OF THE HIGHSTREET

Here we are. Bennett's Bookshop. The only bookshop this side of Milton Keynes.

You could be anywhere once you're in here. When you're inside you don't have to know that you're in crappy old Greysworth. You don't even have to know that you're a sixteen-year-old girl with a wonky fringe and occasional acne breakouts; you can just live somebody else's adventure. You can live in somebody else's world.

Bennett's has this smell: the dustiness of the old wooden shelves and that papery smell of new books. It's defo in my Top Ten Smells, somewhere with petrol stations and new shoebox smell. It's cool and dark in here, a proper oasis away from the *buzzing metropolis* we've left outside, and is closing early for 'staff training purposes'. Me and Holly make our way through the maze of shelves and head upstairs to the staffroom as Maxine politely asks the *only* customer in the shop to leave.

'Hey, Adam!' I whisper, as I creep alongside one of my favourite Bennett's full-timers.

'Hey, sit here.' He pats the plastic chair pulled up next to him. 'How are you doing?'

There's a paper plate of Mr Kipling Cherry Bakewells untouched on the coffee table. Usually free cakes don't last *seconds* around here; what's wrong with everybody?

'Umm . . . okay . . . a little confused . . .' I look around for a clue as to why everyone is so tense in here. 'How are you?'

He scrunches his nose. 'I'll be fine.' His eyes are closed as he says it.

'Psssssst!' Holly squeezes onto the same tiny plastic chair as me and glances at Tony. Like we're in school and hope the supply teacher won't notice that we've got one buttock per person squashed on to the seat. 'What's going on, Adam?'

'I don't know any more than you do.' He looks away from us and watches a guy in a suit who nods towards Tony once it's confirmed that we are all here. He can start.

'Right, as you all know, my name is Mick Morgan.

I'm the regional manager for Bennett's Book's Midlands branches . . .'

I've literally never seen this guy in my life before. Ever.

Glad that thought was just to myself and not out loud. Adam would have literally killed me for using 'literally' incorrectly.

Tony's arms are folded and he stares at the worn used-to-be-blue carpet. He looks very uncomfortable.

'. . . I'm afraid I'm here with bad news today. I have a statement from head office that I have to read out to you, so I'll go through this and then I can try to answer any questions you have at the end . . .'

My colleagues shift uneasily in their chairs.

Holly squeezes my left elbow and Adam exhales.

'*As you will know, Bennett's Greysworth has been underperforming over recent years. Despite the efforts from staff and numerous customer service initiatives directed by head office, Bennett's Greysworth has failed to improve on budget.*'

Failed. Ouch. This can't be good.

'*With the landlords of the shop keen to demolish and redevelop the property into "multiple state-of-the-art retail units" head office does not see a realistic future for Bennett's Greysworth in a location that will inevitably* become unaffordable. It is with deep regret that I am here to inform you that Bennett's, Greysworth branch, will be closing.'

Crap.

'You will receive individual letters explaining how much redundancy pay you are entitled to. You will be asked to work four weeks' notice and will be granted any time off required for job interviews.'

Four weeks?! Is that it?!

Nikki, one of the women who works here full-time, is crying. Her big eyes are watery and the corners of her mouth turn all the way down.

Adam's eyes are fixed on his battered-up Vans.

Maxine glares back at Mick Morgan, who looks very sheepish, and Tony pipes up.

'I'm so, so sorry about this, everybody. I'm so sorry we couldn't make it work.'

We couldn't make it work.

What about our little bookshop family? Surely this can't *actually* happen.

'I don't like this any more than you lot do. It's heartbreaking to see another Bennett's close. Just another casualty of the high street.' Our regional manager shakes his head. 'It's not the nineties any more. People just aren't buying books in the way they used to.'

Those words hang in the hot air of the overcrowded staffroom. I look at Tony, who clenches his jaw.

Tony's been here the longest. Apparently, Adam told me, he's approaching his *twentieth* year here. Which is too crazy for me to get my head around. He's been here longer than I've been *alive*. So while my milk teeth were falling out at birthday parties in Pizza Hut or The Funky Forest soft play area, Tony was here. While I cut myself shaving my legs for the first time, Tony was here. While I had my braces put on and while I had them ripped off three years later, Tony was here. Demolishing Bennett's would be like demolishing Tony.

Yes, he's perpetually in a foul mood. No, he's barely spat two words at me since I started working here, but he *did* give me and Holly jobs, and, who knows, maybe seeing the way 'bookselling has changed' has made him the troll he is today.

'I'm going out for a fag,' Maxine declares as she leaves the staffroom, evidently wounded by Mick's news.

'I think we could all do with a cuppa,' Nikki says as she blows her sad nose into an already-cried-in tissue. 'Who's up for the Bridge Cafe?'

Mick looks relieved that it's his cue to leave and he

gathers his stuff at the same time all of us do.

I look at the gloomy faces around me and I can't take it any more. I have to say something.

'Well, *I* think we should stop Bennett's from closing.'

BOOKSHOP TOSSERS

Mick Morgan gazes down at me wearily.

'And who are you?'

'I'm Paige.'

'*You're* Paige. Paige Turner! When I saw your name on the payroll I thought *surely that's a pseudonym*!'

Okay.

So, if my life was some cheesy sitcom, this is the bit when I'd click my fingers and everyone in the frame would freeze on the spot. Mick Morgan would be mid-LOL JK at that complete and utter *eye-roll* of a line and Holly would be stuck cringing at that being the billionth time she's watched me endure it.

My name is Paige Turner. It hasn't *always* been my name. I don't *really* have the cruellest parents in the world. I was born Paige Campbell back when my mum and dad were happily married. Then when I was thirteen they got divorced after Mum found out Dad had been having a six-month affair with some chick he worked with. I obviously took my mum's side, and changed Campbell to her maiden name – Turner – in solidarity. I know it's a stupid name, but I did it for my mum and I'd do it again. Even though it means I face the lifetime inevitability of Christmas-cracker-worthy jokes from guys like Mick.

Our gang of reject booksellers, and Mick, are making our way to the front door of the shop.

Every town has a Bennett's. Just like every town has a Shoe Zone or a group of panpipe-playing buskers. If we go, then all this town centre will have left is . . . discounted shoes and panpipers.

'Really, though, even if it means *chaining* ourselves to the shutters, they *can't* close Bennett's down.'

'Yes, Paige!' Holly is behind me, sliding a paper plate of Mr Kipling cakes into her bag.

Mick Morgan grimaces, like all this talk of action is making him uneasy.

'Someone should do something . . . *We* should do something!' I stomp my foot. I physically *put my foot down*.

'I guess that someone could be us . . .' Adam laughs.

We answered an online quiz last week that revealed we are *BFF*s (Best *Frolleagues* Forevs). Basically that means that we are friends who started off as work colleagues. I was buddied up with him on my first day. We bonded over a mutual love of sixties girl bands as he trained me on the tills and warned me about the weirdest customers I'd encounter. He makes the best playlists and we play them through the ancient speakers when we're on shifts together.

'What should we do?'

We gather outside the front of the shop, where Maxine points a manicured nail in the air. 'I'm calling a Disgruntled Bookseller Meeting! The usual table at The Bridge. I'll be off to buy more fags first. All are welcome to attend.' She glides past us all and heads to the corner shop up the road, her straight grey bob disappearing along the high street.

Mick raises his eyebrows at Tony. 'Good luck, mate.'

Tony looks incredibly uncomfortable. It's pretty obvious to me that they are anything but mates. That if Tony had Facebook (if he was, like, fifty years younger) he wouldn't even *respond* to a friend request from Mick.

'Best of luck to all of you. Any questions, drop me an email.' Mick waves a thick hand in our direction and off he goes.

I know we shouldn't *shoot the messenger* or anything, but I'm defo imagining shooting him with one of those Super Soaker water pistols that have made every summer of my life an older-sister hell. I'm thinking water guns, but I'm pretty sure Tony and possibly Adam are fantasising about real bullets puncturing the back of Mick's shiny suit.

We stand around as Tony rolls down the metal shutter. It's an old shutter, not like the one they have across the road at JD Sports. They just press a button. Tony has to wind this Victorian-style lever thing around until it rolls down. It's an effort. He's working up a sweat. Unlit cigarette balancing between his lips.

The thought of looking for a new job around here is worrying. Mum was made redundant four months ago and isn't having any luck finding something new. I *need* to work so I can save up for uni. I'll take out a student loan, but from what I've heard that will barely cover my rent. I can't stay here forever; without a job I'll never afford to escape. As Tony wrestles with the shutter, I glance at the empty shop units along the high street. There's nothing else here.

A couple of topless lads stride past and snigger, shirts hanging from the waistbands of their football shorts. One has a particularly bad case of bacne, which isn't his fault obviously, but people in glass houses and all that. He cups his hands around his mouth and shouts, 'WAHEEEY, BOOKSHOP TOSSERS!'

Hilarious. Even Tony laughs. He drops his fag out of his mouth and it lands on the pavement. The really scummy part of the pavement by the shutters that always looks wet, even today when it hasn't been raining. All eyes are on him to see whether he'll pick it up and put it back in his mouth. There's no way I'd eat or smoke anything off this street. The three-second rule does *not* apply.

Way too gross.

It kinda looks like he's considering it.

Just then I hear knocking. Banging on glass.

It's loud.

It's coming from the window.

There's someone in the window display, trapped inside the shop.

'Oh Christ, that's all we need!' Tony's ready to explode as he starts frantically winding the shutter back up.

The lurker moves towards the door and is on the other side of the glass as Tony struggles with the ancient shutter.

It slowly reveals two feet. Big feet, boy feet, in battered old brogues. They look like they're dusty and splattered with paint. White paint, fleshy pink paint.

The ankles are bare and skinny.

Two long legs. Two legs that seem to go on for miles. Black jeans, ripped on one knee, but not the kind of rip that Topman cut into their clothes on purpose.

Holly giggles and Adam tuts, but I need them all to shut up because something huge is happening here and I'm not sure what it is yet.

I'm well aware that my mouth is hanging open. I'm catching flies. I can't tear my eyes away from the Big Reveal behind this shutter.

It gets stuck and Tony motions for Adam to give him a hand. 'As if head office aren't giving us enough grief already! This is *exactly* the kind of thing they expect from our *underperforming* branch!'

Tony isn't even muttering any more. He's pretty much wailing. And I can *see* the sweat on his head.

The more the shutter rolls up, the hotter I feel. Sweaty and cold at the same time.

The boy behind the glass is not the kind of crusty nose-picker we usually find around here.

He's kinda cute.

In fact, he's very cute.

He's tall and his shoulders hunch slightly. His hair is dark and thick and longish but not *long* long.

Tony yanks the door open and spits, 'What do you think you're doing?!'

The Boy speaks and time stands still:

'I-I'm sorry, I've just been here reading. I didn't realise you were closed.'

He pushes his hair back when it flops into his eyes. In his other hand he holds a large hardback.

It's a book on Egon Schiele. Ooooh. Freaky nudes. Yes. Oh God, yes. I want to talk. I want to tell him about how much I love Egon Schiele's portraits. About how I wrote an essay about him before Christmas for the Art History module we did with Mr Parker and how isn't it crazy that those paintings were done such a long time ago but really not a lot has changed. Bodies still look like bodies, right? I want to talk. I want to say so much. I want to ask him who the hell he is. But I'm stunned. Well and truly stunned into silence.

'Didn't you hear the announcements?' Tony isn't taking this well.

The guy shrugs and shakes his head. His beautiful head.

'And you didn't think it was odd that all the lights just turned off?!' Tony's ready to blow.

'I'm sorry.'

The boy looks over at me and when we make eye contact

17

it feels like I've stuck my fingers in the sockets and pulled the hairdryer into the bath all at the same time. Wow.

'Why didn't you just get out when we told you to?!'

I'm totally looking him up and down. This is shameless. If I was some creep at a bus stop behaving this way, I'd totally tell myself to get lost right about now.

Nikki puts her hand on Tony's shoulder, like she's some East-End barmaid preventing a punch-up in the Queen Vic.

'I think you should leave.'

'NO!'

For a split second, I'm not certain whether I said 'no' out loud or just thought it in my head.

But then Holly starts creasing up and Adam frowns a 'what?' at me and I realise it wasn't inside my head; it was out of my big fat lips and audible.

The Most Beautiful Boy In The History Of The World walks along the high street; away from me as Tony asks if that was a friend of mine.

'No. No. No, I mean, *no, Bennett's can't close*. That's what I meant when I said "no", so –'

Tony exhales dramatically and picks the cigarette up off the ground. Oh God. It's *well* beyond the three-second rule now. He holds it to his lips and lights it up. None of us are willing to challenge or ridicule him on this; we just watch in disbelief as he turns back to the shutter.

'Did you just *see* that?' I claw on to Holly's wrists as we walk, wanting confirmation that I didn't *imagine* that beautiful, mythical creature of a boy.

'Ummm, *yes*, who *is* he?!'

'*He* is – I don't know who he is! But I have to find out! Where did he *go*?'

'Did you *see* that way he looked at you? OH EM GEE.' Holly swoons as she slumps onto the side of the sculpture monument thing outside the empty BHS.

'What? How did he look at me?!' I didn't imagine it! I didn't imagine it!

Holly does her best impressions of him swinging his head round to me and doing some intense stare. It's ridic but it's hilarious.

'Oi, c'mon, you two!' Adam reminds us, calling from the gaggle of booksellers trudging in the opposite direction.

SUGAR TEARS

We file into the Bridge Cafe. There's wooden panelling and framed landscapes on the walls. And wipe-clean seats and artificial flowers in vases alongside bottles of ketchup and mayo. It's familiar. It's just up the road from Bennett's. It's The Place to gather for a WTF-Just-Happened meeting.

We're hit by that fatty smell that when you're starving smells delicious, but otherwise is just pretty gross. The kind of smell that makes you try hard to breathe through your mouth and think about washing the clingy stink out of your hair as soon as you get home.

I'm not hungry. This is rare. I'm ready to blame my lack of appetite for fried things on the sad circumstances that brings us all here. I mean, it's a massive shock so it must be that, right? It's not that since that ABSOLUTE BEAUT of a boy looked me RIGHT IN THE EYES my stomach has felt like it's been flipped upside down. Like that feeling you get when you drop from the highest point on a Thorpe Park rollercoaster.

'To Bennett's!' Bruce, one of the Bennett's old timers, holds up his mug of builder's tea to make a toast.

'Twenty years . . .' Tony speaks to the table. His head is propped up by his elbows. 'Twenty years . . . to become a *casualty of the high street*. . .'

Holly insisted she was 'too devastated to possibly order a milkshake' but lo and behold, within seconds of mine being slammed onto the tabletop, her Rimmel London lips are slurping on my straw and she's downing my drink.

'But we can't just *let* this happen!' I say.

I don't know what would happen if Bennett's actually went. I can't imagine any shop that would take its place. In fact, the saddest thing is that maybe *nothing* would take its place. The high street is made up of more empty units than open shops. Is there really a queue of businesses lining up to pay an even higher rent to a swanky new space?

And if Bennett's Greysworth was to go, then we'd have to get a *train* to the nearest bookshop. And I wouldn't get a staff discount or first dibs on any of those books. I wouldn't be able to sit behind the counters in those bookshops, pretending to actually enjoy coffee and dipping into a book that makes me look sophisticated and intellectual.

Holly's Best Mate Telepathy kicks in when she whines, 'We can't close now – the third and final book in the *I'm a Murderer* trilogy isn't published until the end of the year, and I *still* don't know who the murderer is!'

Holly's into really gory crime thrillers. Even more so since we started at Bennett's and she's had open access to all those books that are banned from our school library.

This shop has been part of my childhood for as long as I can remember.

I think about all the Christmas book tokens I've splurged there, the hours I spent with Holly on the way home from school. Part of the reason we were employed at the same time was because Tony couldn't tell us apart; he'd only seen us together. 'Joined at the hip.' We'd sit back to back reading passages from saucy romance novels to each other until we'd be interrupted. Then we'd try to look sensible, which is way harder than it sounds when the last words you uttered were 'throbbing member'.

I shake away that thought as my colleagues round the table talk. Holly pours low-fat sweetener on the table and moves it around with her fingers making it into the shape of a sad face. Sugar tears.

Throwback to when we received phone calls from

Bennett's to say they wanted to offer us part-time jobs. It was almost too good to be true – being *paid* to spend time in a bookshop, with my best friend! We danced in the corridor at school and Bitchy Mrs Bradley swung the music-room door open and told us to keep it down, didn't we have revision or something more important to be getting on with? We didn't revise that night, instead we bought a huge bag of candyfloss and scoffed the lot until we felt like we might be too sick to turn up for our first shifts.

'C'mon, you lot . . .' I start up again. 'Didn't you hear what Mick-whatever-his-name-is said? We've got four weeks before they kick us out and knock the place down. So we've got *four weeks* to do *something* to change their minds . . .'

Adam winces. 'Do you really think anything we do will change their minds?'

Tony isn't joining in. He drains the last bit of his coffee and gets up to order another.

Bruce raises his eyebrows. 'It could be worth a try . . .'

'*Thank you, Bruce!*'

'We don't exactly have anything left to lose, do we?' Maxine agrees.

'It won't be as easy as you might think, Paige. It's all about money. The landlords will make more of it on rent once they've got us out of the way and built some flashy new units . . .' One of the blokes who works Monday to Friday tries to reason with me. I didn't expect everyone to be so negative. So afraid that we could fail.

'Well, okay . . .' I place my hands on the sticky tabletop, to try to get my thoughts in order, and I instantly regret it when the vinegary residue sticks to my palms. 'In an ideal world, who would want to stay at Bennett's for longer than the next four weeks? Raise your hand.'

Eight out of eight isn't bad.

'Okay, so, let's *say* something, publicly, about staying open. Let's tell people that we don't want to leave.'

Tony glares at me. He looks . . . *irritated*. Like I'm saying all of this to cause trouble in some way. I'm not. I'm trying to save his shop. *Our* shop.

'It'll work out. We can work it all out.' I nod, trying my best to reassure him.

Holly shouts out 'Yeah!' in BFF solidarity.

'We could do something, I'm not sure what yet, but like a protest, or a petition –'

'A petition would be good.' Adam nods in agreement.

'We can't be the only ones in this town who don't want to see the back of the bookshop . . . Think about all of the regular customers –'

'Why not?' Bruce's smile is wide and I catch a glimpse of the tooth he's missing towards the back of his gums.

I'm scribbling all of the ideas that are flooding my brain into the pink Moleskine notebook I keep in my bag. Adam and the others are feeding me with suggestions, and eventually I work up an appetite and order a plate of chips.

I might just be the bookshop girl with a bad fringe, who's using books to jump into other peoples' lives. Maybe nobody cares about what *I* think, but if there's a whole *group* of us, who all stand up against what we think is unfair, then we'll be impossible to ignore. We should be loud about our plans. We should tell everybody what we think. We should save our bookshop and our jobs. *We should do something.*

SERIOUS FITTIE

My phone pings. I had no idea it was that time already. A text from Mum flashes up on my screen asking if I want a lift home. She's finished her CV-writing workshop. It's this class she has to do to qualify for her Jobseeker's Allowance. I jump out of my oilcloth-covered seat for a chance to bypass a blistery walk.

'See you tomorrow then, Holly-wood!' I blow her a kiss while she squeezes a sachet of ketchup onto yet another bowl of chips.

Texting Mum to say I'll be there in a sec, I navigate my way past the hair extensions and heels and eyelashes and bad tattoos and aftershave and *sorry darlin'*s along the pavement, feeling like I've successfully managed to indoctrinate the others with my vision of a Bookseller Uprising.

I hear the car before I see it. Mum's sitting in the Fiat Punto with windows rolled down and 'Ghost Town' by The Specials blasting full volume.

When I get in the passenger seat she turns it down. 'Hey, baby! How was your day?'

'Hmmmm . . . Well, some random bloke in a suit came to tell us that they want to demolish Bennett's.'

She twists the volume all the way down in disbelief. 'You are joking?!'

'No, really. But it's all going to be fine, because we're going to make sure they can't close us down . . .'

'Oh, Paige, that's such a shame. It would be terrible if it closes. There's nowhere else to get books around here. And y'know what I heard today? Right, listen to this: the council are making cuts so the library will be closed on *weekends*! Can you *believe* that? It's disgusting. People *rely* on that service.'

I stare out of the window, at TO LET signs plastered on every other empty shop unit along the Welly Road. Some joker has been at every one with a spray can and added an 'I' in the middle, so now they all read 'TOILET.' I snigger while she's mid-rant.

'It's hardly Banksy, is it?' Mum LOLs at her own joke. 'At least we could keep each other company, y'know, glamorous mother-and-daughter trips to the jobcentre!'

I picture the two of us in fluffy white robes, kicking back on sunloungers and sipping champagne while we have our nails filed and make a long list of our transferable skills.

No way.

I *have* to do something about Bennett's.

At home, Elliot rushes to the front door to let us in. He's a few years younger than me and still finds running around outdoors fun. He's been playing football in the park all day, and hasn't changed out of his muddy shorts. His game of *FIFA* is paused on the TV screen and he's halfway through a tube of salt and vinegar Pringles. Hashtag living the dream.

'That was here for you when I got in, Paige.' He points to a padded brown envelope. I clutch it to my chest, already knowing what's inside. Another chunky prospectus from another university. I'm collecting them. Arty courses up and down the country. I don't know where I want to go yet, but I still have an excruciatingly long amount of time to decide. At the moment I'm coveting these brochures like they're sacred texts, keeping them all together in an old plastic toy box in my room.

'Thanks, Elliot!' I dash upstairs and shove the envelope under my bed. Saving it for later.

Through dinner and through *University Challenge* and even when we hear the ice-cream van chime some dodgy version of 'Greensleeves' as it does a U-turn in our road (and Elliot asks if we can get something and Mum says, 'We've got choc ices in the freezer if you *really* want an ice cream,' and neither me nor my brother is surprised because it's a tale as old as time) That Boy, who was locked in the shop, is in the back of my mind. Moving around my head on a loop like an overused GIF. I keep going over the moment we both looked at each other and remembering how it felt. Like a scene on *24 Hours in A&E.*

They'd slide me out of a stretcher and onto a table where people in plastic disposable aprons would rush around me and cut off my jeans and apologise for ruining my clothes and I'd be, like, 'It's okay,' as I'd stare up towards the ceiling with my head in one of those neck-brace things and a paramedic would be, like, 'This is Paige Turner; she's sixteen years old. After a collision with a Serious Fittie she's suffered a cardiac arrest. She's a casualty of the high street.'

BOOKSHOP GIRLS GET BUSY

I snap a twig off a bush and scrape it along the wooden fences as Holly and I walk side by side and she tells me about this morning's panic-fuelled job hunt.

She raises her hand to her forehead, all damsel in distress. It's not the first time I've considered what a good Shakespearean actress she'd make. I've seen her do a mean Lady Macbeth monologue on a particularly dead Sunday-afternoon shop floor. 'Job hunting is *bleak*. Seriously, I was so determined to hand out all the CVs I printed last night; I tried everywhere! I –' pause for dramatic effect – 'I even went to the *Games Workshop*! *That's* how desperate I am for cash.'

'That's a new low,' I remark, thinking about the reek of sweaty pubescent lads that pumps out of that place.

'Nowhere would take my CV, though; they just looked

at me like I was a sandwich bag of fresh dog poo.' She pinches the bridge of her nose and impersonates a snotty shop assistant. '*All applications are online* . . . Eugh, I was so desperate to get rid of the CVs I stood above the bowl of the Grosvenor Centre loo and was seriously considering flushing the lot.'

'Don't worry, you won't need to hunt much longer, Hols, because our petition will do something to *stop* us losing our jobs!'

I should really be tired. I'm what snarky Physics teachers who catch you yawning at the back of the lab would class as 'sleep-deprived'. I was up all night watching YouTube clips and reading books from work about people (mostly women) who have campaigned and protested for things they believe in and *actually been successful.*

Women who have set up online petitions to ban topless women from so-called 'newspapers', to scrap the tampon tax or the closure of women's refuges. I clicked link after link after link.

At one point, around three o'clock, I felt a bit stupid. Like, this is just Bennett's Bookshop in Greysworth, right? Will anybody actually care if we lose our jobs?

I looked at myself, sitting there, sweating in a heap of blankets, mascara smeared all over my tired face, and I felt kind of silly for thinking Bennett's closing was in *any way* linked to the protests these amazing women were organising.

Then something caught my eye. My bookcase. My wonky, wobbly bookcase. It's not a trendy, neatly stacked IKEA unit like Holly's; it's pine and it's unfashionable and it's rammed with books I've collected since I was tiny. Beatrix Potter books I scribbled in with felt-tips, the Rumpelstiltskin picture book that scared Elliot so much he threw it down the toilet. My copy of *Pippi Longstocking*. My fave. I remembered Mum buying me this *from Bennett's*. I thought about how I'd spent hours copying the illustrations of Pippi lifting that great big horse above her head. Pippi was a little girl, but she was fearless.

I don't know if it was the lack of sleep or the amount of time I'd been staring at my laptop screen in the dark, but I felt so emotional, and before I knew it I was seriously beginning to ask myself, 'What Would Pippi Do?'

It was just like that scene in *The Lion King* when Simba sees Mufasa's face in the clouds. I could see Pippi Longstocking's mad, freckly face in an imaginary Disney cloud surrounded by stars and she was telling me to believe in myself. To believe in the campaign! To go for it! To lift Bennett's Bookshop way above my head! That we *have* to fight for smaller things too. Smaller battles have to be fought for so that bigger changes can happen.

I may or may not have been crying at this point. I *was* definitely crying when I played 'Can You Feel The Love Tonight' seven times on a loop (through my headphones so Mum couldn't tell me to calm down and go to sleep).

One of the things I realised around four thirty was that protests are *rarely* covered on the news. I guess that's so bumpkins out in the sticks like us don't get any ideas about joining in with protests or thinking we could change things. Watching all of these videos made me so excited. Made me think that actually I *could* make a change. Not alone, but with the others. With everyone from Bennett's. It made me feel like if we came together and told people about why we should get to stay open in Greysworth, then maybe people would join us. And if a load of us came together and made a point, then surely we couldn't be ignored, could we?

This is Something. I mean, how often does anything *happen* around here? What have I even got to lose? There's *eff* all else to do before we go back to school anyway.

POSERS

Well, I guess there's one other thing to do. Mr Parker says that we can get extra marks for our Art coursework if we include life drawing in our portfolios. He reckons drawing the figure from real life is always better than copying from magazines or photos. The only thing is, because we still legally count as minors (eye-roll) the school rules say that there cannot be ANY NUDITY UNDER ANY CIRCUMSTANCES ON SCHOOL PROPERTY. So while we've had a few Art lessons drawing each other fully clothed, Mr Parker suggested we find some real naked life-drawing classes to go to in our own time over the holidays. Immediately I was really up for this. I'm not entirely sure why. Maybe it means I'm some sort of pervert . . .

Anyway, I found a class at the uni here that's on every

Tuesday night. It runs all year round but anyone can join any time they want. It's called 'Posers'.

Luckily Holly was a keen bean too. So here we are, trekking across the park towards the campus, sketch pads and pens and brushes and inks stuffed in our bags. Backache dot com.

'D'you think we'll get a fit life model?' Holly asks, her eyebrows triangular with excitement.

'I doubt it.' My automatic know-it-all response kicks in, although I really have no idea.

'Mr Parker said it's more interesting to use models who are old, or really overweight, or really skinny, because there's more bits to draw, like, more details and shadows and wrinkles. He said when he was at art school they had disabled models with wildlife documentaries projected over their bodies. Apparently it's cool to paint that.' She shrugs like it's the first time I've heard that, which is nuts because I was sitting right next to her in class when Mr P told us all about his life-drawing days.

'Well, seeing as skinny pensioners with feathery skin are your thing, you could be in for a real treat!' I do my best dirty-old creep face.

'Hubba-hubba!' We are already squawking uncontrollably as we trudge through the grass and up to the art school. How the hell will we behave when there are genitals on show?

We push through the doors, still high from our fit of LOLs and step into the foyer. It's dark and quiet, and inside glass cases there are bits of work on display. A clay sculpture of a woman's head. A dress made of recycled plastic bottles.

'Oh, it's through here.' Holly points a chipped purple nail to a handwritten sign for LIFE DRAWING THIS WAY.

We walk through a maze of corridors. It's the summer holidays so the studios are mostly empty. Rows of abandoned sewing machines and easels in room after room. Then we walk past an open door where a radio is blasting a Taylor Swift song and there's a group of women in overalls screen-printing.

Holly's starts singing along to Taylor as we move down the corridor and I join in. 'Shake it off! Shake it owwwwwwf!' We're shimmying along the hallway obliviously when all of a sudden a man's voice cuts into ours.

'Oh, look at this, it's the Spice Girls!'

The two of us grind to a halt.

'Wow. The Spice Girls. Pur-lease. Last time I heard that I fell off my *dinosaur*,' Holly whispers pretty loudly in the direction of my ear.

'We're just on our way to life drawing,' I try to explain.

'Well, you've come to the right place, ladies. I'm Clive – I lead the class.'

Clive is in his late fifties, maybe early sixties. I'm so rubbish at guessing age. My mum takes it as a huge insult when I describe someone as 'really old' and she discovers they're younger than her. Clive IS old, though.

He's head to toe in beige. Beige hair, beige skin, beige shirt hanging over beige combat trousers, then beige lace-up shoes. Beige. Is that not the most offensive colour? Is he doing it for the irony? I don't know. I do know that I take an immediate dislike to anyone who is fully clad in beige and addresses me and my friends as 'ladies'.

'We're about to get started in a few minutes so find yourselves some room and get settled; I'm just popping out for a snout.' He holds a cigarette up to us in his beige fingers.

It's not a big room but it's got high ceilings and about six other people in there. Mostly smiley middle-aged women who all seem to know each other. One is in a purple dressing gown, eating a pear and chatting to a lady in corduroy.

There's a mattress on the floor with a few battered old

scatter cushions and one of those portable heaters pointed to it. This could all easily seem a bit seedy.

Holly and I aim for spaces at the back, behind a lad our age, who's dressed in sportswear. He's good looking, in a boy-band kind of way. Like, the bad boy from the boy band. If it was the nineties and he was the bad boy of the boy band, he'd have his eyebrow pierced. But it isn't so he doesn't. He looks up and says a steady 'Hey' when we squeeze past him.

I start unpacking. Miffy pencil case and brand-new sketchbook. First-day-of-term vibes. I really hope we don't have to show our work to the group. Everyone here seems so at ease and like they know what they're doing. I'm already cringing and I haven't even started drawing yet.

Clive returns, grin on his face. 'Okay then, gang.' He's rubbing his hands together with glee. 'We've got a few new faces here tonight, so I'll go through how we usually do things here at Posers.' This is a guy who likes the sound of his own voice. 'Sue is our model tonight. She'll do a few poses for us; some will be ten minutes, some will be a bit longer than that. Is that all right with you, Sue? Back not giving you too much trouble tonight?'

Sue nods in agreement, already stepping out of her purple robe like it's completely *normal*.

'We don't show our work after every pose but if you're happy to at the end of the session, we can share. Oh, and we do have a fag break, and teas and coffees halfway through. Right then, ten-minute pose, please, Sue.'

The room falls silent. Clive stands at his own easel and starts waving his right arm around straight away. I look over at Holly and we do our best to suppress our immature smirks.

I pick up a pencil and try. Sue's body is interesting to draw. There are bits where she sags, and her skin stretches, and bits where the knobbly bits of her spine jut out. And the hair. Like, the *pubic* hair. I'm not used to seeing that on TV or in magazines. Those bodies are always so smooth and even and not really like my *or* Sue's bodies. Would she be offended if she saw our drawings of her? Would she be upset of we drew her nose really big or her boobs really small? I guess not. I guess you've got to be brave to sit naked in a room full of strangers when you know for a fact that everyone is paying close attention to how you look. The funny thing is that after a while, it really doesn't seem so strange that she's naked. It's pretty much like the six weeks of Art GCSE we spent drawing wax fruit.

I'm just adding some shade to Sue's nipple when the

door creaks open. Someone's coming in late and she doesn't even flinch. What a pro.

Holly grabs my arm and I look up.

Jesus Christ. It's Him.

A FIT, ARTY, OLIVER TWIST

OMG. It's HIM. It's the cute guy from work. The one who got locked in the shop yesterday. The lurker. He's here. He's where I am. Here. We are both here.

'Sorry I'm late, Clive.' He doesn't whisper and his low, even voice breaks the silence of the room.

'S'all right, son, come in!' Clive whispers back and waves him into the room with his thick beige hands.

Son?! Son? Is he Clive's son?! No way!

They don't look alike.

I mean, okay, not everyone looks like their dad.

I don't look at all like my mum. She has naturally black hair, and mine is fair, slightly gingery, but she *is* actually my mother. Like, there is proof somewhere that she pushed me out and into this world. (She loves to go into detail about the birth. '*It was like squeezing a melon-sized object out of a lemon-sized hole.'* Ew.)

Not everyone looks like their parents. But Clive, *really?*

Could this boy really be the fruit of Clive's loins? Did that melon-sized head squeeze through a lemon-sized hole that Clive has come into contact with?!

He clocks me. Eye contact. I'm going to be sick. Right here. Right now. Sorry, Sue, it's not you, it's me. I can feel Holly watching as he walks past everyone in the class and makes his way to the back of the room.

To the back of the room next to me.

There are no more chairs left so he picks up a weird tall wooden stool thing and sticks it beside me.

'Hey, you're the Bookshop Girl.' He smiles as he says it, like he *knows* he's melting me from the waist down.

I want to say many things. Like '*Hey*' and '*So you got locked in my bookshop last night. That's pretty funny, right?*'

My bookshop? What am I saying 'my bookshop' for?! Like I'm a kid who refers to the slide in the park as 'my slide'. For God's sake, Paige, shut up.

'Yes.' It's all that actually comes out of my mouth and I leave it at that.

Just take another glance at him.

Maybe Clive isn't his dad. Like, maybe Clive's the kind of man who calls younger boys 'son' even if they aren't biologically linked.

I'd hate that aspect of being a boy. People calling me 'son' left, right and centre. It would really creep me out. No one really calls girls who aren't their daughters 'daughter'. But I suppose people do refer to girls in all sorts of other mind-numbingly idiotic ways to make up for it.

He catches me staring at him. *Crap.*

I never knew my cheeks were this flammable. I'm a fire hazard. I'm burning up. My face is ablaze.

He pulls out a tin of inks and nibs and starts scribbling in his sketchbook. I suddenly become very aware of the nipple I've been circling with lead.

I turn to Holly.

'*OMG! OMG!*' she silently mouths over and over like she's about to pop with excitement. We can't get carried away, not now.

Maybe Clive isn't his biological father but he has raised him. Maybe he took him in when no one else would. Maybe he's an orphan. Like Oliver Twist. Like a fit, arty Oliver Twist. And Clive raised him. And he comes here to draw naked Sue because Clive is his legal guardian.

Of course. The book he was reading. The Egon Schiele nudes. It all makes sense. He's an artist. He's an artist. Oh God. He's a beautiful, struggling, *orphan* artist.

How long are you an orphan for, though? You can only be an orphan when you're a kid, right? Because he is defo not a child. He's a man.

Okay, well, not a Man-Man. But he is not like the sixth-formers I see walking home from the boys' school. There's not a hint of bum-fluff baby beard growth on his face. He's older than me. By a couple years I reckon.

'Lovely, Sue, could we have another ten-minute pose now?' Clive clears his throat then nods in her direction.

Sue's bones crack when she takes a standing position. I try so hard to focus but as I tear the last sketch from the top of my pad The Boy leans in and takes it. WTF!

'You have good line.'

Eff off! Did I say you could look at that?! How rude.

But.

Those eyes. So big and blue and open and I don't think he's taking the mick. He's not smirking, or laughing – and I *do* have good line.

'Thank you.' It's all I can muster. I am so embarrassed and annoyed at the same time. I don't want him to look at everything I draw. I'm suddenly so conscious of my 'good line', of the heat in this room, of all the nudity. My head is spinning. *Do not pass out in here, Paige. I repeat, do not pass out.*

I take a sip from my water bottle to try to compose myself and when I go back to drawing I turn towards Holly, away from him, and cover my work with my arm like I'm doing a Maths test in Year Four.

I just cannot concentrate. I feel like someone has taken a putty rubber and erased the contents of my brain. I've lost my artistic ability and the physical function of swallowing. Did I actually just dribble? Oh God.

He smells good. Like soap and fags and boy. I know that might not seem like a good combo on paper but I am *intoxicated*.

'Thanks, Sue, that's great.'

Has it been ten minutes already? How? I look at my paper and flip my book shut before he gets his hands on it.

'Shall we take that break now, guys?' Clive stretches his arms up and yawns. Beige sweat patches. 'Let's give it fifteen minutes then meet back in here.'

Before I know it That Beautiful Boy is up and out of the door, cigarette balanced between his beautiful lips.

IN THERE LIKE SWIMWEAR

'OH EM EFFING GEE.' Holly's jaw drops and she tosses the fine liner into the air for dramatic effect.

'He said I had good line.' I look over to the mattress, where Sue is lying on her stomach eating a custard cream and chatting to corduroy woman again.

'You *do* have good line. He must come here. He knows Clive.'

Of course. He goes to uni here, that's how he knows Clive. Obvs Clive isn't his dad.

'He *clearly* fancies you!' Holly *is* the emoji with heart eyes. 'You are *in there* like *swimwear.*'

I take another swig from my bottle. *Cool down, Paige. Be cool.*

'Let me see what you've done anyway. It's a good class, right?' I change the subject and Holly passes over her sketches.

'I like it here,' Holly agrees, 'although I wish we had a bit longer on each pose. As soon as I get into it, it's time to change.'

Sue takes a gulp of her tea and asks, 'So what are you girls studying here?'

Wow. Sue must think we're students. I'm so desperate to pose around at art school that being mistaken for an actual student makes me feel like I'm one step closer to that dream becoming a reality.

'Um, we don't go here. We're at the girls' school,' Holly answers. And then clarifies, 'Not the posh one.' It's true. We attend the school that saw the famous Flaming Sanitary Towel Bomb incident of '99. Before our time, but scorched into Greysworth Secondary School folklore.

'So you're on your summer holidays now? All that free time to get up to all sorts of mischief I bet.' She winks.

'Well, we work in Bennett's Bookshop in town, so . . .'

'Oooh, bet that's a nice place to work.'

'It is! But it's actually closing down . . .'

I start to explain but Sue spits her tea back into the home-made ceramic mug she's drinking out of. 'No! When? How?!'

'They want to demolish us and build fancy new shops in our place.' I pause. 'But they won't.'

'Hey, that's the stuff, girl!'

'We're setting up a campaign to keep it open.' Talking about it to someone I don't know makes it feel so real. 'A petition.'

'Good for you, girls . . .' She starts talking to her corduroy friend, who's ferreting around in her trolley of art materials, but as she speaks she doesn't take her eyes off us. It makes me laugh nervously. 'Did you hear that, Elspeth? They're closing Bennett's, knocking it down?' She shoves the remaining half of the biscuit in her mouth, talking as she chews.

'No, what are they doing that for?' Elspeth squints through her glasses and looks to me for an answer.

'They want to bulldoze us out and build brand-new shop units, which Bennett's won't be able to afford to rent.'

'These girls are starting a petition.'

'Ahhhh, great! That's what we like to hear, new Posers *and* activists!' She beams. 'Well, you can count me in.'

'Me too! I love Bennett's. It's the only place in town they'd let me breastfeed my Dominic when he was a baby . . .' She's reminiscing and then adds, 'I'm sick to death of shops closing in this town.'

I remember all the TOILET signs by the empty shop windows and laugh on the inside.

'So is it an online petition then?'

'We haven't actually set it up yet . . .' Holly starts and I jump in.

'I was thinking we should wait until we're all together at work to do it properly.' I'm well aware that the four-week deadline to turn this round is already creeping nearer and nearer, like a dreaded Maths exam or TB jab.

'I'm always getting emails from one of those online petition sites . . . Which one was it?' She stares hard at her unpainted toes, straining to remember, while the two of us wait politely. 'I signed something to stop the disability allowance cuts . . . Oh, what was it called? It'll come to me and I'll let you know. There's a few of those sites around now, you know for all the *clicktivists* out there . . .'

Sue excuses herself to go to the loo and, I wish I didn't, but I spend some time thinking about how she'll have to wipe really thoroughly to make sure that no little drops of leftover wee trickle out when we're all watching her. Not saying that she's incontinent, or that *I* am, you just wouldn't want that to happen in a public place with all eyes on you, right? *Right?*

'What's a clicktivist? What's click-ti-vi-sm?' Holly concentrates like it's a tongue-twister.

I shrug. She takes out her phone and Googles.

'Ahhhhh . . .' she whispers knowingly under her breath. 'It's basically using the internet to run campaigns and petitions.' She scrolls. '"*See also: Slacktivism*".'

'Aha! I think I might be a slacktivist,' I confess.

'I'm a *snack*tivist!' Holly pulls a cereal bar out of her bag and I roll my eyes at her *grandad-worthy* joke.

The second half of the class is a blur. A hazy blur of nipples and Him and cheeks and Him and hands and Him and Sue and Clive and Him. When Sue is lying on her side, one leg up in the air (I know right, *ambitious*) he leans over to me whispers, 'Hey, try this –' He holds his hand out to me.

I just take it.

I take his hand in mine. And for a millisecond it's beautiful.

Until the pencil in his hand jabs my palm and it's awkward and, Oh My God, what just happened? I grabbed his hand. He was passing me a pencil, clearly that's what he was doing, and I felt him up. Okay, brilliant. Okay, I take the pencil. Should I even be allowed out? I might ask my mum to lock me under the stairs. It could probably be a huge benefit to man-and-woman-kind if I was just stowed away in some kind of Harry Potter cubbyhole.

'Sorry, thanks.' It looks like a normal black pencil. It says CHINAGRAPH in silver writing along the side. It has a few teeth marks at the top of it. His teeth. He bites his pencils. Bet he bites the tops of pens too. Bet those beautiful lips of his have been stained by accidental blue ink before. Why is the thought of that making me so hot?

I press into the white paper with his pencil. His chinagraph between my fingers. If I bit the end like he did, it would be like our teeth had touched.

It's not like a normal pencil at all. The line is thick and black and heavy and greasy. Not oily like pastels or shiny like graphite. My 'good lines' look better in this. I become so excited by this new discovery and by how it makes my sketches look that I get really into the drawing. It's his pencil. He's right there. He is so beautiful. He has excellent pencils. I press too hard and it snaps. Loudly. Eyes in the back row are on me. Holly and The Boy look over. Face. Ablaze. Again.

'I'm so sorry. I'm really sorry, I didn't mean to, I –'

'You're a monster!' The widest grin spreads across his face. It's infectious; I have face ache from smiling.

'I didn't mean it . . .' I'm laughing. 'I just – I'm sorry, I got carried away . . .'

He laughs too loudly and that's when Clive holds up

his hand and says, 'All right, quieten down over there now, please.'

He leans over again and whispers, 'Have this one. But please, be gentle.' Another chinagraph. Brand New. No bite marks.

So now he's moved closer to the mattress to get a better angle of Sue. Looks like he's really focusing on her feet. He's spending a long time on getting the tonal qualities of her toenails down onto paper. Maybe he's a foot pervert. He might have a foot fetish. I'm not a great fan of feet. Even the TV screen in Boots that shows the demo videos for the JML Ped Egg makes me feel a bit queasy. But I bet his feet are *delicious*.

He really frowns when he draws. And he hunches his shoulders right into his sketchbook.

I know this because he's kind of directly in front and a bit over to the side of me.

Sorry, Sue, no offence but, like, I'm kind of wrapped up in this guy right now. I'm actually drawing him. I'm observing him. And I like what I see.

SHOW & TELL

'Okay then, thank you, Posers. Thank you, Sue, for being our Poser tonight. What we usually do now is lay our work out on the floor, the piece you're happiest with, and then we'll just take a look around and discuss bits.' Clive must see the panic in my expression. 'No pressure.'

No! I completely forgot he said we'd show our work! Otherwise I would not have spent the last twenty minutes salivating over That Boy. Well, I might have done, but I wouldn't have *drawn* him.

Right, I'll show the chinagraph drawing of Sue. That'll do. I fold the other sheets of paper away inside my sketch pad and leave them on my chair.

Holly's favourite bit of work is her purple ink painting. Streaks of ink have run in some places but that makes it look cool, like it's moving. She bites her nails anxiously.

The boy-band lad lays his work down. He's stuck a pencil behind his ear and his work is the strangest. He's used bright pink and yellow felt-tip pens, and where Sue's breasts should have been he's written TITS; where her bush was just says GASH. Not in any type of fancy writing, just in his simple, bold, handwriting.

Holly scowls and mouths 'WHAT THE HELL?!' at me.

Clive holds his chin and comes to this one first.

'What's your name, mate?' So he's a newbie too.

'Jamie.' He's got intense dark eyes but the rest of his body looks completely relaxed, like it doesn't bother him one bit standing here talking about why he'd write those words over Sue's body. Sue is standing here right now by the way. Dressing gown on.

Clive laughs kind of nervously 'Go on then, d'you want to tell us about it?'

'Yeah, well, basically it's just, like, this is what a lot of lads see.' He pauses. 'Or are told to see. Birds and Tits and Gash. It's objectification. I just drew that objectification. Commenting on women's bodies is considered a social norm. I was just thinking about that as I was drawing. About how we label women as parts of their bodies. And actually labelling this portrait looks crude and nasty cos it is.'

I think about that white van hurtling past me on the

way to Bennett's yesterday.

There's a moment's silence and Jamie looks around the room at the rest of us, then Clive puts both hands to his chest and exhales dramatically.

'Phew! I'm glad you said that, mate. I was bricking it for a minute. What does everyone else think of this?'

'I see what you've done and I think it's a very brave approach.' A super soft voice. Like triple-velvet toilet roll. Sue's friend. Elspeth. 'These words are obscuring the body. As viewers, we are unable to see past these words.' There's a general census of approval from the group. Holly's face has relaxed and she looks like she is more than a bit impressed with his explanation. Nods and 'hmmms' and more chin holding. 'Other than the words, your proportion and perspective are spot on.'

'Cheers!' Jamie looks genuinely humbled and happy with the response. We go around the room and chat about each other's work. It's actually a nice process. Everyone is learning together, even if some of them are old-timers.

'This chinagraph piece is beautiful.' Clive frowns as he compliments my work. 'Whose is this?'

I raise my hand and look over at The Boy who is smiling without looking at me.

'Fantastic. The weight of the line is handled very well.'

'Thanks.' I am so thrilled with Clive's feedback. This is better than any Art class at school with Mr Parker, that's for sure.

'Do you work with chinagraph a lot?'

'Um, no, it was my first time.' The Boy looks down at his shoes and his hair falls into his eyes and I can actually feel my knees melt all the way down into pools in my shoes.

'Wow. It suits you. Did you use it all session or did you change materials?' He holds his chin as he looks at me.

'I . . . I changed. I was using pens and then . . . I changed . . .'

'Great! Do you mind if we have a look at your work from earlier in the session? I just love chinagraph and you've done such a good job that I want to compare the way it really lifts the line. It would be great to compare it to your other sketches –'

No no no no no no no no no no no no no no no.

He is in there. I repeat. The boy I'm obsessing over is in that sketchbook. No.

'No.'

'Sorry?'

Oh God, I said that out loud, didn't I?

'I spilled some inky water over my other work, so, sorry

56

but it's gone forever now.' I'm grinning like a complete nutter as I say this and grab the sketch pad so no one can possibly get to it. I see the realisation set on Clive's face, like, *Oh, right, she's insane. I guess I'll move on.*

'Okay. Okay, let's look at Elspeth's work –'

I don't really pay much attention to the rest of the class. I'm clutching the sketchbook filled with images of Him close to my chest. And every now and then I think about how the tiny paper versions of him are nestled up flat against my bosom. Like some kind of voodoo doll that could be used to get him on my body. *No, Paige, focus!*

'Right, thanks then, gang. Great work. Thanks for joining us – hope you'll be back next week. Same time, same place.' Clive claps his hands together and smiles.

We start to pack up and The Boy turns towards me, shrugging back into his leather jacket.

I smile. With my mouth closed. I smile with my mouth closed because I feel like if I don't, there's a good chance I might projectile-vomit all over him.

'Bye.' One word. Totally, one hundred per cent directed straight at me. One word, especially for me.

'Bye.'

He folds his sketchbook shut, tucks it under his arm and leaves the studio. Oh, to be that sketchbook, nestled under his armpit . . .

'Girls, here it is.' Sue bustles over, squinting at her phone screen. 'I've got it up on here, one of the petition sites I was telling you about . . .' She scrolls and sticks her tongue out slightly as she focuses. 'Here . . . Make a Change dot org.'

'Oh great! Thanks, Sue!' I make a note of the address on my phone.

'It's such a good idea, so easy to just click and support something . . . not like the old days when we'd be standing out in the freezing cold with a spray-painted bed sheet, trying to get passers-by on the high street to care.' Elspeth chuckles. 'It was fun though.'

'Oh, and this one's good because – look –' Sue holds the screen up to show me and Holly. 'It says here that if you reach one thousand signatures, then you can expect a response from the local council.'

'Great!' That could be just what we need to save Bennett's.

'You can count me in, once you've set it all up . . .'

'Yeah, there's a few things we still need to figure out, but we'll get on with it ASAP!'

'Make sure you're clear on the people you're addressing it to.' She widens her eyes to demonstrate the seriousness of what she just said. 'Y'know, those landlords, the council who are prepared to demolish the place, this is about telling *them* that *you* are not happy with that decision . . .'

'Yes.' I scribble what she just said onto the corner of my sketchbook to make sure I don't forget it.

'Next week, when you're back here, send us all the link and we can help you save your bookshop.'

'Thank you so much, Sue.' I genuinely mean it. I think Sue might have just become one of my favourite people.

'And thanks for letting us draw you!' Holly gushes. This Sue crush is A Thing now.

'Ha!' She throws her head back when she laughs and her whole body jiggles. 'Any time! You made some lovely work, you girls. Have you never done life drawing before?'

Holly, the other half of my Bookshop Saving Girl Gang, gets chatting about art and school and Mr Parker, and I'm kicking myself for glazing over just above Sue's shoulder as she talks, wondering where That Boy went off to.

NOT NECESSARILY
CLOSING DOWN SALE

'Oh for God's sake!'

Tony presses the bridge of his nose with his thumb and forefinger. Holding the huge flat envelope that he's just opened.

'Head office have had these made up.' He passes Maxine the post and she pulls out several banners. Ugly red letters shout 'CLOSING-DOWN SALE! EVERYTHING MUST GO!'

Wow. And there it is. The reality that everything must go. Including all of the little booksellers farting around in here.

'We're not putting them up,' Adam states defiantly.

'We have to,' Tony grumbles.

'No.' I snatch them.

'Paige, give those back.'

I ignore Tony and scramble to grab the nearest pen to hand. Luckily it's a thick black Sharpie.

'If we *have* to put them up, then we can at least alter them slightly so that they're not *misleading* . . .'

I kneel on the floor and scrawl 'NOT NECESSARILY' across the top of the first banner I get to, asking for clarification on how many 'C's and 'S's I need to spell it correctly.

Adam claps, then grabs a dark green marker pen to customise the other posters in the stack.

I underline 'NOT' twice and it's more satisfying than I ever could have imagined.

'There!' I get up off the floor, dead pleased with myself.

Tony tries not to laugh as he jangles his keys and mutters, 'Bloody hell . . . we'd better open up . . .'

The NOT NECESSARILY CLOSING-DOWN SALE posters have given me an extra kick up the bum. The clock is ticking.

'Today we should set up the online petition. Who's with me?!'

Tony rains on the parade. 'Please don't forget to stay on top of your usual duties though. We've still got a lot to get through and I don't want you to get all wrapped up in this petition thing and forget to do what you're here to do.'

I roll my eyes and I know he catches it.

'Erm, excuse me . . .'

I look up from behind the desk, where I'm creating an account on Make a Change. Oh God, it's Mr Barnes.

'Have you got any books about *Coronation Street*?'

Come on. Eyes *off* my chest, please. It's the same every time with this guy.

'I'll have a look for you.' I run a quick title search on the computer. No results. What a surprise. 'Sorry, no we don't have anything in.' I force my best Customer Service Training Happy Smiley Face even though this bloke gives me the Creeps with a capital C.

He comes into the shop, like, every Saturday and has been in trouble a few times for 'shoplifting'. Well, his poor attempts to shoplift. Stuffing books down the front of his trousers. For all to see. And walking very slowly towards the door. How much of a loser do you have to be to steal books from a place like Bennett's?

As he shuffles away from the till and makes his way towards the Fitness & Health section I slump back into position behind the counter. There, I carry on with the first draft of our 'Save Bennett's Bookshop' post.

It's actually a bit busier than usual in the shop today,

and I have a bad feeling it's to do with the SALE banners in the windows. The upstairs part of the shop that usually only seems visible to the weirdest portion of Greysworth's population has attracted a wider audience today.

A woman in cropped jeans with flashy sunglasses stuck on top of her head shouts across the shop floor to the counter. I can only assume she's talking to me.

'Is this reduced as well?' She waves a self-help book in the air.

'Yes. It's half price now,' I answer.

Without reacting out loud to what I've just said, she produces her phone and squints at the screen. I know exactly what she's doing.

'Ah, it's actually cheaper online. I'll leave it.'

Adam moves next to me and recites his favourite Bennett's catchphrase quietly in my direction. 'Every time you say "online" in a bookshop, a kitten dies.'

Even though that's one of my fave Adam lines, I'm slow to laugh and he asks if I'm feeling okay. It's unlike me to not crack up.

I'm just tired. I had another late night. Pouring over the sketches I drew of The Boy. Just like I have been doing every night since Posers. I'm aware that makes me sound like an utter psychopath but there's no other trace

63

of him. Even with Holly trying desperately to track him down, so she won't be beaten on the 'Pro-level Online Stalking Abilities' she proudly brags about. This boy has zero online presence.

Those sketches are all I have.

Well, those and the chinagraph pencil.

It's like the scarf at the end of *The Snowman*. It's proof that he did really happen. I didn't just dream him up. I don't want reality to mirror everyone's favourite Crimbo tearjerker too closely, though; I don't think I could cope with standing in the garden, in the snow, in a pair of slippers, crying at a pencil as The World's Saddest Credits start to roll. Merry fudging Christmas.

'Hey, Adam, look.' I invite my frolleague to read the computer screen with me. 'It says there is usually a five-to-seven-working-day response rate for petitions that reach one thousand signatures.'

That means we have to gain as much support as we can, in an even *shorter* amount of time. Less than three weeks to collect a thousand signatures and hear back from the council.

'Wow. Okay, we'd better get cracking then!'

Just a few more clicks and 'Yep! We're live! It's up there!'

He crushes my hair as he hugs me but I don't mind.

'Yes! Okay, I'm going to send it to everyone I know!'

'I'm going to print out copies of the link to the site and we can slip them inside all of the books we sell. Like bookmarks.' *I'll make sure that no one leaves this shop without knowing about the petition.*

'Yes! Good idea!'

It's actually happening.

'Ooooh and we should send it to all the other branches of Bennett's!' Adam moves onto the keyboard and starts clicking.

I dig around under the desk to load more paper into the antiquated printer. When I'm down there, I notice something I've never seen before.

'What's this, Adam?' I trace my fingertips over the biro words that have been scratched into the old wood.

Somebody has scrawled '*ONE DAY I'LL WRITE A BOOK ABOUT THIS PLACE.*'

And below it, another hand has written '*NO ONE WOULD BUY IT.*'

He crouches down beside me to have a look. 'Oh, that. That's been here for ages. I don't know who did the first bit . . .' Then he smirks. 'But I will take credit for the response.'

I crack up. 'No way! It's always the quiet ones!'

IT MIGHT NEVER HAPPEN

Lunchtime. I walk through the shopping centre. Right now some ancient eighties power ballad is ringing out of the tinny speakers. There are only about four tracks on a loop, echoing around the empty units and last few crappy shops that remain.

I printed out more of the #SaveBennetts petition bookmarks and am carrying them like a bouquet of flowers in my hand. Armed with some cute sparkly tape, I plan to stick these babies around the town centre for all to see. For all to *hopefully* see, since the black ink in the printer is obviously low and the letters look unintentionally stripy.

I spot the community noticeboard between Superdrug and the entrance to the bus station. I find some space among the ads for garden furniture for sale, childminders for hire, and an urgent appeal for donations to the food bank. I stick a few of our flyers on there, careful not to cover the poster for a missing cat. I'm not sure if anyone actually reads this, but it's worth a try I guess.

I also need to find a present to take to Lucy's party tonight. It's her birthday. I don't really know what to get her so I play it safe and follow my nose all the way to Lush. I figure I can kill two birds with one stone; surely the happy vegan babes would be sad to lose Bennett's, maybe I can get them to sign the petition. I'm pretty sure they wouldn't approve of me killing any birds with a stone so scratch that. I'm going in.

I pick out a pink heart-shaped bath bomb and a bubble-gum lip scrub, and the frizzy-haired shop assistant wraps them up in spotty tissue paper.

I take the paper bag and the shop girl flashes her perfect teeth between two orange lips, painted in animal-friendly organic lipstick. I pluck up some courage. 'I was just wondering if I could leave some of these here on the counter?'

She reads the slip and I continue, 'I work at Bennett's Bookshop on the high street, and it's facing closure and then demolition in three week's time.'

She pouts in sympathy.

'It would be great if you and your friends could sign and share the petition to keep us open?'

I smile as she says, 'Yes! Of course I will! Thanks . . . and good luck!'

It feels really good telling people about the campaign. People I don't know, *strangers*, who are willing to help. I practically skip out of Lush and back through the shopping centre, passing flyers to shoppers and lunch-break shop assistants, who sip icy Pepsi from Burger King straws as they tap the petition address into their phones and sign up to support us.

Holly bursts through the staffroom door chanting a school-disco classic as I'm stuffing my bag back into my locker.

I sing right back at her. We're so musical. Our talent is wasted in this town.

Nikki raises her eyebrows behind the latest issue of *The Bookseller* magazine and sighs. Insert Haters Gonna Hate meme here.

'So, I wasn't sure what to get Lucy so I just went to Lush . . .' I'm already tearing the tissue paper open to show Holly.

I hold the bath bomb up to her nose. Too close. I accidentally bash her in the face and leave a pink chalky stain on her cheek.

'Ow!'

The door swings open and Tony's in the room. Why is it that he only ever catches me when I'm behaving like a complete weirdo?

He looks at his watch. Then at me. Then at the clock on the wall. Guess that's my cue to get back to work. Yes, okay, I took an extra three minutes off the shop floor. He looks at me all expectant, so I tell him all about my lunchtime flyering sesh. He grunts. Unimpressed.

I have pink, glittery bath bomb residue all over my hands but I feel like if I spend any more time up here and not downstairs selling books, Tony will actually explode.

Back on the shop floor, things seem to have got a little trashed by the customers that have descended on our NOT NECESSARILY CLOSING-DOWN SALE. Adam stands behind the till with this :-/ expression on his face.

'Paige, you're not gonna like this.' He holds up a can of polish and a yellow cleaning rag. 'Tony asked if you could give the shelves a dust. I'd do it if it wasn't for my allergies.'

I think Adam's expecting me to moan. I'm battling with the urge. Instead I just take the cleaning products from him. It's okay, I'll dust, doesn't mean I'll do a good job at it. I'll just dust near Adam so we can chat.

'So, Adam, what are your plans for this eve?'

'Well, I'm going to the pub with a couple of mates for a few drinks. Although I'm trying to cut down on drinking; it's bad for my anxiety.'

Poor Adam is an anxious man. Don't imagine that all this bookshop-closure-possible-unemployment chat has been doing him any good. He rubs the back of his neck with his hand and changes the subject. 'What about you?'

'I'm going to a birthday party.'

'Aww, how sweet. I remember birthday parties when I was your age.' He stares into the middle distance and his eyes mist over behind his glasses, like it was centuries ago when he was a young lad. I let him have these moments. It's a lesson to myself that as I get older, I'll make a conscious effort to never do the 'when I was your age' thing to other people.

I tiptoe to sweep a thick layer of dust off one of the higher shelves. It gets into my eyes and I rub it away but IT BURNS. I forgot I still had pink Lush product all over my fingers. Now it's clogging up my left eye. The pink Lush bath bomb and the bookshelf dust. And the polish. My eye is streaming. It's like there's something huge and sharp in there. Like I'm being stabbed in the eyeball.

'Are you okay, Paige?' Adam is genuinely concerned.

He should be. I'm going blind over here.

'There's something in my eye . . . It's really sore.' How embarrassing, now my nose is running too.

'I'll get Nikki, she'll know what to do.' She's a trained first-aider. Brilliant.

I stand still and blink, all too aware that my black mascara and eyeliner are running into the cocktail of things destroying my vision.

Before I know it, she's here shouting 'Can you hear me, Paige?' into my ear.

YES, I CAN HEAR YOU, NIKKI. LOUD AND CLEAR. I'M NOT DYING.

Or am I?!

'Okay, let's have a look then.' She moves my hands away from my face and produces a torch. Really? Wow.

'Yes, I see, you've got something nasty in your eye. Let's go upstairs to the ladies and get your eye washed out.'

In the toilets she tends to my eyeball, as I pull the lid high and look up, down, left, right and up again until it feels clear.

'You're going to have to take your eye make-up off, Paige.' Said just like a teacher who sticks to the school policy on nail varnish in food-tech classes.

I look in the mirror. My left eye is nearly completely closed and there's black eyeliner all down my cheek. I look like a Tim Burton character. *Happy Halloween.*

Nikki watches my reflection in the glass. 'Well, I've already signed. And I've handed plenty of those web address slips out . . .'

I sniff all the goo back up my nostrils and smile as I scrub my dirty cheek with balled-up toilet roll and water. 'Great! Thanks, Nikki.'

She pauses in the doorway to offer some advice before heading back to the shop floor. 'Chin up!'

Adam physically jumps when I reappear on the shop floor.

I know I look a mess but *ouch*.

He scuttles off for his break, which means I'll actually have to interact with customers while he's away.

Mr Barnes, the guy who likes to shove stolen books down the front of his trousers is here for his second visit of the day. I tell him about the petition to save Bennett's. I figure he might like to know that we might not always be here for him to nick things from if he doesn't support the cause.

Ancient Bennett's regular Mr Abbott is sitting in his usual spot by the window. He stares out onto the shop floor and smiles to himself. White beard and flat cap. I've already attempted to strike up a convo about the campaign but he responded in the only way he ever does. He frowned and asked if we have any books on the German navy.

It's kind of apparent that he doesn't actually *want* the books he asks for. It's as if he can only find the same few words muddled in his head, and they're the ones that come out. 'Pig farming' or 'beard lore' or 'German navy' or 'cherryade' every time. But props to him; he's the only person so far to be completely unfazed by my Lushed-up appearance.

In the distance I see That Boy appear. The beautiful one from life drawing. Oh My God.

Oh, but my stupid *eye*! I can't let him see me like this.

I crouch down and hide behind the promotional life-size Mary Berry cardboard cut-out, clutching the piece of loo roll that I've saved for any more eyeball leakage.

He glances around, like he's looking to see if anyone's about. Like he's looking for me?! Maybe he has come here to see me again. Why does he have to be here now, when I've been bath-bombed?!

I watch him from my secret hideout.

He picks up a book of Victorian medical illustrations. I *just* shelved that today! I basically put it right there, *in his hands.* That's it – we are meant to be!

I clench my fist into a silent *yesssssssss*, when all of a sudden somebody stands over me and totally blows my cover. 'Excuse me?'

Eff Eff Ess.

I stand up and turn to the woman who's asking for help; she recoils at the sight of my gammy eye. 'Oh dear, is your eye all right there, love?'

I ignore her question and smile manically, clinging on to my cardboard wingwoman. 'How can I help?'

She's looking for a Spanish phrasebook, so I tiptoe her to the right shelf, pleased that The Boy still hasn't clocked me creeping around.

Quick! I drop to the floor to crawl back to my hidden lookout.

I'm.

Too.

Slow.

'Hello?'

I freeze. On all fours. In the middle of the shop floor.

I turn. It's Him.

'*Hey!*' I try to say it dead casual, like it's normal to come across a sixteen-year-old girl crawling on the carpet like she hasn't grown out of playing 'CATS' just yet.

'What are you doing?' He laughs as he asks, and the dimple of his cheek *nearly* stops me from coming up with this corker.

'Oh, I'm just here . . . just fetching this –' I feel around the carpet, and pick up a lump of spat-out chewing gum *in my bare hands*.

Kill me.

I don't know where this gum came from, I don't know whose mouth it was chewed up in, but it's still wet and it's in my hand and I am talking to The Most Gorgeous Boy In The World and I ONLY HAVE ONE FLIPPING EYE.

'Oh, right. Great.' He must wonder how he's stumbled onto the set of a particularly cringey episode of *The Undateables*. I jump up and flick the sticky gum off my hand and into the recycling bin behind the counter. Gross.

'Sorry about that! Hey!' I try to smile and feel the lid of my dodgy eye get stuck. Oh God. I think it just looked like I winked at him. Who *winks*?

'Are you okay? Your eye . . . it looks . . . painful . . .' he asks. Concerned. Oh, how sweet! And how embarrassing!

'Yeah, thanks.' That's it? That's all I'm saying? Apparently so. Fantastic.

The Boy picks up some of the Save Bennett's flyers on the counter. He pouts and I die.

'Is it okay if I take some of these?'

I nod uncontrollably like the Churchill car insurance dog.

'It's an online petition, right?' His face is serious and looking right at me for answers.

I'm massively annoyed at myself for glossing over the campaign like its no biggie, just because I feel so awkward in front of him right now.

'So you're an activist?' he asks, raising his eyebrows.

I laugh. Is he joking? What a funny question. 'Um, well, yeah, I suppose this campaign makes me an activist . . .' He isn't laughing. 'Are *you* an activist?'

More pouting. 'Well, I've been to a few demos and protests in London. I'm an activist, yeah. I'd like to think of myself as an "anarchist". I believe in absolute freedom of the individual.'

'Cool!' I gush. I can't pretend that I'm not shamelessly impressed by everything he does. He's a beautiful, arty, freedom fighter who's been to *protests* in *London*.

'So, yeah. I'd like to get involved,' he offers.

This is so special. He's supporting *my* campaign. He's showing an interest in the most important thing in my life right now and the whole time I'm dying at the injustice of this magical moment happening when I look like a creation from a special 'Swamp Creature' themed episode of *RuPaul's Drag Race*.

I make an excuse to hide again. 'I should really get back to work . . .' I lie. Like I'm going to be able to do anything but obsess over this encounter.

'Oh, okay. Well, count me in. With the petition. Or whatever.'

'Cool. Thank you.' And then I ask because I've been dying to know since I saw him locked in the display window. 'What's your name?'

'I'm Blaine Henderson.'

Wow.

A first *and* last name for me to fancy.

'I'm Paige. Turner. Paige Turner.'

'Well, I'll see you later, Paige Turner.' He untucks a freshly rolled cigarette from behind his ear and leaves.

Some old codger shuffles up to the desk and croaks, 'Cheer up, love! It might never 'appen!'

Eugh! I hope Lucy enjoys her Life-Ruining Bath Bomb.

SWEET SIXTEEN

In a highly flammable cloud of perfume and hairspray, Holly and I find ourselves standing outside The Plough. It's a pub. Lucy's hired the function room at the back for her Super Sweet Sixteenth.

I've had most of my birthday parties at home. Caterpillar cake and party bags with mood rings and Smarties in them. As much as I loved those parties, and Holly's birthday sleepover where we wore matching onesies and ate twice our body weight in Domino's stuffed-crust pizza, there's something exciting about getting ready to go out-out.

We wouldn't get in to any of the clubs in town, so a private function room in a stuffy old-man pub may be kind of lame, but we're treating it like we're superstars, about to be papped on the red carpet. About to have 'Who Wore It Best' articles published about us. About to spark new trends and hashtags as the whole world hangs on our every move.

Hol pushes me to go in first, her freshly manicured hands flat on the back of my charity-shop gown.

That's right. I said gown.

We've gone all out. Like it's prom night at the end of one of those American high-school films.

I found this nineteen-sixties lurex number in Save the Children. I ran my fingers over the silvery pink floral pattern and (breathing through my mouth because we all know chazza shops can stink) clutched it close to my heart. It was love at first sight and hands down the best tenner I've ever spent. At Holly's house we watched make-up tutorials online before gluing on false eyelashes and backcombing for eternity.

'The Look' is High Glamour (despite the fact that the location is more . . . High Cholesterol).

The stained-glass door swings behind us and we're inside the main bar.

We stand momentarily, taking in the shimmer of fruit machines and the stale smell of soggy beer mats.

Below a hand-painted chalk board advertising 'Fish Fridays', a couple of crusty old blokes with about four teeth between them turn round on their barstools and leer at me and Holly.

I fold my arms across the top half of my body, all too aware that their bloodshot eyes are boring through the artificial fabric of my party dress.

''Ave a good night there, gels!'

Groan.

People with a higher tolerance to men-saying-whatever-the-hell-they-like might think *Hey, y'know, it's just some old guys being nice, what's wrong with that?*

I have nothing against people genuinely being nice, but I do have a problem with the fact that they probably wouldn't turn to a group of sixteen-year-old *lads* and say anything. We're being treated in a certain way, just because we're girls. The best thing to do is to ignore it, right? Avoid making a scene. Don't make them feel uncomfortable, even though the way they look at us is pervy enough to make us squirm.

It's a typical example of male privilege. The assumption that they can say whatever they like to girls. The assumption that women or girls are there for their entertainment.

Funnily enough, when I was doing my hair and squeezing into my outfit, I wasn't doing it for *their* benefit.

Holly takes my hand as we follow the sound of '*DJ Dave wishing Lucy a Happy Sixteenth Birthdaaaay!*' through the double doors in the back room.

DJ Dave is exactly as you'd expect him to look. He's wearing one of those short-sleeve shirts with flames on it. He nods his balding head to the beat as he stands among the menagerie of pink helium balloons, cheese and pineapple sticks, sausage rolls and red velvet cupcakes.

The party hasn't quite kicked off yet. It's just the birthday girl's family here so far.

'Happy birthday, Luce!' We greet her with hugs and I hand over that lethal bath bomb.

'Thanks for coming! Hopefully it'll get busier soon . . .' She looks pretty nervous at the possibility that the party might *not* get busier soon. But it should; according to the event page on Facebook, pretty much everyone from our year group is coming tonight. 'Help yourself to some non-alcoholic punch!'

While DJ Dave is playing some party bangers, we decide we'll add a bit of the peach vodka Holly snuck in in her bag to the very, very sugary punch before we join Lucy's granny on the dance floor.

It's not long before the room is filled with girls from school. We take selfies in the toilets. We screech along to 'The Grease Megamix', portable disco lights flashing green, then pink, then yellow onto glittery plastic princess crowns and ironic transfer tattoos.

We shout over the music to tell classmates about the online petition and happy-clap as they get it to load on their phone screens and sign up. We sit around a plate of cocktail sausages, elbows leaning on a paper tablecloth, as we listen to a detailed and gripping account of how Hannah Matthews lost her virginity during the hols. We gush over Netflix box-set binges, run our fingers through new haircuts and hiccup uncontrollably because of all the peach vodka. We're girls, at a party and we're happy. In this crappy room in this crappy pub in this crappy town, we're together and we're having a flipping ball.

SUNDAY MORNING

This is not good. It's Sunday and I'm covering Adam's day off so it's just me here on the first floor. I really don't feel like working when my only company for the day will be the mother of all hangovers.

I just want to curl up by the graffiti behind the counter. My head is pounding. And my teeth are fuzzy. And I feel hot and cold all at the same time.

Oh, I'm so sweaty. This is grim. If I wanted to go for Binge Round Two right now I could. I could just wring out my clothes and drink the sweat. I'm pretty sure that the alcohol volume of my sweat would be enough to get drunk on all over again. I really *don't* want to do that by the way. In fact, I don't want to drink ever again. That's it. Paige Turner is going sober at the tender age of sixteen. I can't let another drop of peach vodka touch these lips.

No.

Oh God.

I'm on my hands and knees behind the till.

I'm going to vom.

On all fours.

Right here. Right now.

I can't make it upstairs to the loo.

I panic and grab a small carrier bag.

A large! I need a large!

What if someone sees me?

The shop floor is dead and the security cameras haven't worked the whole time I've worked here so just go for it.

Oh God.

No.

'Paige? Are you okay?'

I scramble to my feet.

Blaine!

Beautiful art school activist Blaine is back! He's come back to see me again!

'Hi! Hello, Blaine!' I'm very aware of the sweaty film glistening on my upper lip. I can see it. I can see it shine.

'How's it going?'

'Yeah, good than—' I feel something rise in my throat and swallow it back down.

My eyes are streaming. I just blink. Blink it away.

I stand there trying not to make any sudden movements as he runs his fingers through his hair and asks how the petition is going. I feel like he's finding excuses to talk to me but I can't be sure. Is he really this interested in the campaign to save Bennett's? Or is he interested in *me*? I wonder as I stand holding the bag I was nearly sick into.

'The petition? I'll just have a look online . . .' I tap on the keyboard and log in to the Make a Change site, thankful that I have something to do, something to distract me from just staring, mouth open, at Blaine's face when he's so near.

'Wow!' The signatures are really adding up. We're already near the halfway mark. 'It's going really well!' I beam and my stomach happy-flips, rather than hangover-flips.

'You've signed up, right?' I ask.

'Oh, yeah. Did it straight away.'

'*Amazeballs.*' Did I really just – Yep, I really did say that.

He nods, and some lad walks over, *interrupting this special moment*, and asks if I have a bin, so that I can dump his empty cup. I say yes (as if I'm some kind of *slave*) and take it, even though the waft of strawberry milkshake makes me gag all over again.

Back to Blaine. 'Okay, cool. Well, I'll let you get back to work. See you round.'

'Will you be at life drawing on Tuesday?' I ask, praying that the desperation to have him there isn't too obvious.

He nods and walks over to the Art section. I watch as he runs his index finger along the spines of the books and pulls one from the shelf. Dreamy.

Suddenly there's a woman standing at the till with a book in her hands. She wants to pay.

'Hi,' I say in her direction but I don't take my eyes off Blaine. On the Customer Service Performance Charts head office made us fill out a few weeks back, I'd get a red light for this. Tony would not be pleased.

'That's seven ninety-nine, please.' I invite the lady to tap her card, but she insists on using chip and PIN. She's telling me some Tolstoy-length *saga* about why she doesn't trust contactless payment. Not now, love; I don't want to lose him.

There's so much more I could say, starting with '*I don't usually say "amazeballs" by the way. In fact, I've never said it before in my life, until about five minutes ago.*'

Nope.

I'll keep that to myself.

The lady across the counter punches her PIN into the machine as Dreamboy Blaine hunches over a book of Lucian Freud portraits. Of *course* he's a Lucien Freud fan.

Holding the weight of the book in one hand, he raises the other to his mouth. He turns the pages with such care. Oh, to be those pages. He looks so thoughtful. He looks so beautiful. Then he looks at me.

This transaction takes an eternity to go through the till. I wait impatiently for the receipt to print out. I'm telepathically willing it to hurry the *eff* up.

Finally I have it in my hand and pass it over to the customer, while keeping an eye on you-know-who.

'Love you.' It just spills out of my mouth. My eyes snap back to the lady who's paying.

'Sorry, I mean, *thank* you.' Then I laugh hysterically. Too loudly. If he didn't hear me declare my undying love to him then he's defo heard me now. 'Thank you, thank you, *thank you*!'

'Oh! We've only just *met*, sweetheart!' I'm glad *she* finds it funny. I pretend I do too but I can feel my face burning. My cheeks are melting. I fumble around for a carrier bag. Oh God, kill me now!

'Oh no, don't worry, love. I've got a bag here. Save the environment and all that.' Stop! Stop talking. I want to die. She takes her sweet time putting her paperback into her Tesco bag for life and then winks at me before trotting off, still chuckling to herself.

Now what do I do? I must look like a huge embarrassing rash of a human. I look up and he's on his way out. He's walking, pretty quickly, towards the stairs to leave.

I've blown it by being a complete stalker love fiend.

I look to Cardboard Mary Berry for some emotional support, but she's rubbish. Her little raisin of a face just stares blankly back at me.

'PAIGE!'

It's Holly, striding over to the counter. Looking one hundred per cent fresher than she did last time I saw her. She obviously got a few extra hours of sleep and a shower while I've been here ruining my life. 'OMG, have you SEEN the petition?! It's amazing! And it's addictive! I've been watching it all morning, those signatures are really stacking up!'

'Hey, what are you doing here?'

'Oh, well, *it's nice to see you too*!'

I laugh. 'I'm sorry, I'm sorry. It's just today has been *horrific.*'

'You poor thing, having to be here after last night.' She strokes my arm.

I make her stop. 'Hols, Hols, he was just in here –'

'*Who?!*'

'*Blaine!* The boy from Posers. The one, *you* know!'

'Oh my God! He cannot keep away!'

'Well, I doubt he'll ever be back here.'

'What happened?!'

There aren't many customers around and I feel it's necessary to re-enact the whole thing. Holly has to play the part of Blaine so I force her to stand right where he was, just minutes ago. Next to that now sacred shelf.

'LOVE YOU!' I say it loud 'n' clear at the top of my voice and she trumpet-laughs.

Hanging off the shelf, shaking her head in disbelief for what feels like a year, she straightens up and says, 'What book was he reading?'

'Some Lucian Freud one. Hang on. I'll show you.' I stomp round the desk, frustrated that I've just lost this perfect boy, and push past Holly to pick up the Lucian Freud book.

'That's so weird . . .' I whisper as I scan the shelves. 'I can't find it. I'm sure I didn't see him leave with it.' Maybe he paid for it at the till downstairs, too freaked out by my declaration of love to speak to me ever again. I bend to check the lower shelves and all the blood rushes to my head. 'Who knows?! Please just tell me this shift is nearly over.'

LOVE POACH

We trudge along the grass away from the ice-cream van. It's the one parked up by the swings in the park. MIND THAT CHILD and Donald Ducks and Little Mermaids that are all slightly out of proportion, with eyes too close together, painted on its sides. I'm on the look out for a spot that isn't too muddy, or directly in the sun because I'm a Serious Burner.

This heatwave is still at large and I'm still wearing all black everything. Turns out that opaque tights in the height of summer are not at all practical. It probably doesn't look as chic as I hoped it would, when I was getting ready and listening to a mix of French girl bands from the sixties that Holly had made me. I'm a sweaty mess. I'm ready for this ice cream. I need a proper cool-down.

'How many of these d'you reckon you need to eat to get pissed?' Holly slurs between slurps on her lager 'n' lime lolly.

'I probably wouldn't need many to be fair . . .' I admit as I chomp on my chocolate flake and it crumbles all over my dress. 'What's the point in calling this a ninety-nine? Like, when did they *ever* only cost 99p? This was £1.20.'

'Probably in 1999.'

'*It's not the nineties any more, guys!*' My impression of Mick Morgan from Bennett's head office makes Holly choke on the melty lager ice in her mouth.

'Speaking of Mick . . .' I pull my notebook out of my bag and root around for a pen, while trying to stop the ice cream from melting all the way down my arm, with my tongue. 'What's next for the Save Bennett's campaign?'

'We've got, what, about six hundred signatures so far? That's *sw-eeeeet*!'

'Yes! And we have to keep it going . . . I reckon we've everybody we *know*, friends and family . . . We just have to spread it even further . . .'

I eventually find my biro and chuck it on the grass, concentrating on this ice cream. Nibbling round the top edge of the cone. My teeth making marks in the Mr Whippy.

'Maybe we should make a blog or a website or something?' She shrugs. 'Like, we could post updates about the campaign on there, and have articles written by us lot, and supporters of the petition . . .'

'Oooooh, yeah! Like, "I'm saving Bennett's because . . ."!' Cartoon light bulbs and fairy lights and neon signs are buzzing with ideas inside my head.

'We could make videos!' Videos are Holly's Thing. Right now, most of her creative talent is spent on hilarious video montages of her cat Blossom that she uploads onto YouTube. I'm her number-one fan and only subscriber.

I'm chomping the end of the ice-cream cone as fast as I can, so I can write ideas down as she talks. It's so dry that it hurts as I swallow but I don't even care.

'We could record really short and snappy videos of us lot, and customers, saying something about Bennett's . . .' Holly continues, digging the wooden lolly stick into the ground to make a pattern. 'Why they want to keep us open . . . the title of the best book they bought from us . . .'

'Such a good idea! Then we can share it on Facebook, and Twitter, and add it to the petition page . . .'

'Yes!' She claps with excitement. 'Let's tell everybody what we want! Let's shout it from the rooftops!' She's yelling and the women in the distance with pushchairs scowl in our direction.

'We need to direct the link to authors and other bookshops and book-y people . . .'

'We're so on it, Paige!' She chucks the lolly stick and lies on her back, head resting on her arms and soaks up the sun.

'We *have* to get Mr Abbott on one of our videos.' Holly smiles with her eyes closed, still lying in the sunshine. 'He's a Bennett's legend.'

'That shouldn't be hard; he's always there.'

'You know who else is *always* there these days?' She rolls onto her side and looks at me, her face full of mischief.

I giggle. She's talking about Blaine.

'These sightings *are* becoming more frequent,' I agree. *Sightings*. Like he's some sort of fittie Sasquatch or Loch Ness monster. He *is* a rarity, that's for sure. He's endangered. Because I want to poach him. Love-poach him.

'He cannot keep away!' Holly laughs. 'It's you. It has to be because of you.'

'I feel like we have a *connection*, Hols. But, I don't know, why does he always catch me when I'm acting like a total freak?!'

'Well, I hate to say it, Paige, but . . . you *are* a total freak!' She scoffs. 'Jokes, you know I love you.'

'And where has he suddenly come from?! I'm starting to think I've inhaled too much shelf polish and he's just a very vivid hallucination.'

'Ha! Sounds like the plot for a cheesy YA novel.' Her eyes light up and she's on her knees, setting the scene. 'He's the ghost of Bennett's Bookshop, guardian of the shelves, *disturbed* by Mick Morgan and the threat of demolition . . . Now, his only chance of remaining in the literary vessel he has chosen to haunt is to *possess* the young, beautiful, *virgin* bookseller who has captured his cold heart!'

Howling, she falls to the ground. I throw a daisy at her. What a stellar performance.

'Back to mine?' The plan for this afternoon is to make posters and zines and stickers and bookmarks with pictures and collages and #SaveBennetts tags on them to distribute everywhere. They'll be pretty, so people will want to look at them, but they will carry a message and spread the word about the campaign. *Craftivism.* I've got stacks of old magazines and newspapers and glitter glue waiting for us at home.

We stand on the kerb. I press the CROSS HERE button out of habit.

Holly wrinkles her nose and looks both ways at the empty road. Then up at the red man. 'Wait for the green MAN. WTF?!'

I'm not sure where she's going with this.

'I mean, why should I wait for *a man* to tell me when to cross?!'

I laugh with how much I love what she's saying. 'Aha! It's true! I've never thought of it like this before but it's actually a symbol of a man telling us to *stay in our place*!'

'As *if*! We don't need a man to tell us to cross!' She strides out into the road and holds her middle finger up to the illuminated red man on the lamp post. I skip after her swearing at that smug little git as well. Disobedience in the shape of chewed-up pink nails.

A silver Nissan Micra drives slowly towards us and the woman behind the wheel shakes her head at us. Unimpressed. Join the revolution, sister!

'Smash the patriarchy!' Holly yells at the top of her lungs, dead pleased with herself.

On the other side of the road we high five. 'Yes, Hol! Look – we disobeyed The Man and we *survived*! We made it!'

SUSPICIOUS
MINDS

I'm balancing a stack of paperbacks between my upturned palms and my chin, walking very slowly past Tony, who's squinting at an A4 page of numbers.

'You know, we've actually been busier in the last few days than we have been for years . . .'

You don't say. It's been a week since the shop closure was announced and some of the shelves are already looking bare. The books I'm carrying have been picked up and dumped in piles around the carpet. It's like the bargain-hunting locusts have been. I'm trying to tidy what's left and make it look pretty, unloading this stack of misplaced books back onto displays.

'Yeah, I think the campaign is genuinely reminding people that we're here . . .' He frowns and mutters, 'Whether it will keep us open is another thing.'

I steady the wobbling tower of novels in my grip. I fight the urge to fling the book on the top of the pile right at him. I really don't appreciate his negativity. 'Hey, Tony. It's happening. We're going to turn this round. You just wait.'

He raises his eyebrows and exhales dramatically.

'Are they sales figures or something?' I nod towards the sheet of paper he's studying carefully behind his glasses.

'Well, yeah . . .' He sticks a biro behind his ear. 'But it looks like a few bits have gone missing . . .'

'Oh, great. Thanks to that weird guy who shoves our stock down his pants I bet.'

'Mr Barnes? To be honest, I don't think it's him. I haven't seen him around here over the past few days and it's not his usual kind of books that have gone astray . . .'

To be fair, it wouldn't be *hard* to nick things from here, if you have a technique even fractionally better than shoving the book down your trousers. We can't afford a security guard. We *do* however have the poster. Yeah, that poster really means business. It's a photo of a police officer looking cross and it says in big red letters: 'SHOPLIFTERS WILL BE PROSECUTED'. Still, it's a terrible thing to do. If there's one thing Paige Turner does not have time for, it's dishonesty.

'It's the lowest of the low. Only a complete and utter

scumbag would steal from a bookshop that's on its way out.'

'*But –*' I balance the books in one arm, pointing my finger in the air to correct him. 'We're *not* on our way out, are we? We shall not be moved!'

'Are you ready for your close-up, Miss Turner?' Holly appears from behind a shelf, her camera poised; I hope she's already caught me convincing Tony that we mean business.

'Great!' I finger-comb my fringe, which is still embarrassingly short. 'Have you started filming yet?'

'Got a couple of customers from downstairs and Maxine; I need you two next!'

I look at Tony.

'Oh no!' He shakes his head dismissively. 'You don't want me in it.' He's quickly becoming very flustered.

'*Whose side are you on?*' I mutter in his direction, half wanting him to hear, because I do question his dedication to the shop if he's not even bothered about helping us out with the campaign, and half not wanting him to hear, because something about his constant grouchiness is a bit intimidating.

'Of course we want you in it, Tony!' Holly sings. 'You're the *shop manager*! You *are* Bennett's!'

'Okay, all right, well . . .' He pulls at the hem of his untucked shirt anxiously. 'I don't *have* to do it *right away*, do I?'

'*Wrong.*'

Tony blinks at her.

'We don't have all the time in the world. I've got to get as many clips as poss, *then* edit them all together, *then* upload it to YouTube. The sooner we do this the better! The revolutionary clock is ticking! We don't have a lot of time left to reach our target *and then* wait for a response from the council, do we?'

She's right.

'Let's do this thing!' I chant.

'Okay, Paige, you can go first so that, Tony, you have some time to think about what you want to say on cam.'

I make Holly record me three times. On the first attempt I make a weird twitchy smile halfway through, and on the second Mr Abbott, who is sitting a few paces away, farts very loudly, and I'm no way near professional enough to not dissolve into laughter on camera.

I hold a copy of my girl *Pippi Longstocking* up to the lens as I explain that my mum bought it for me, from Bennett's, when I was a kid. It's been one of my favourite books growing up, and I can't help but see it on my shelf and feel a connection to this place. Then I bang on about how books should be available to everybody, and that with the local cuts to library opening times, if Bennett's was to close, it would mean a whole town would be left behind without easy access to literature. And that really the people of Greysworth deserve better than that.

'And *cut*!' Holly gives me a thumbs up as she watches the screen on her mini camcorder.

Tony hovers with a thick paperback in his hands.

'Ready when you are, Tony.' Holly motions him forward.

'My name is Tony Humphreys. I'm the manager of Bennett's, Greysworth. I've picked this book. It's one of my favourites,' he flashes a nervous smile at the camera, '*The Crimson Kingdom* by Hilary Mackintosh. Now, back in ninety-nine, when this was first published, I was lucky enough to be invited to the launch in London, and was able to meet Hilary, who I believe is one of the best authors of our time . . . and, um, well, that was thanks to Bennett's really . . .'

The way Tony goes on to talk about this book shows a completely different side to him. He's almost like the rest of us who work here. Excited and enthusiastic about his favourite writer. Not his normal stressy, stink-eye-shooting self.

I get behind the cash desk, tear a bit of receipt paper from the till and make a note of that name. Hilary Mackintosh.

BLOSSOM'S DEAD.

Tuesday. And for once, *I'm* not the one who's running late.

I text Holly to tell her I'm here. I can hear the muffled steps of someone running down the stairs inside and then her sister flings the front door open.

'Hey, Paige.' She says this looking down at her feet. Christmas slippers in the height of summer.

'Hi, Danielle. You all right?'

'Erm. No. Well, not really. My mum ran over Blossom. She's dead. Holly's really upset but she said you can go up to her room.' She bites her nails and focuses on her wiggling festive toes.

'Oh, I'm so sorry. Poor Blossom.'

'It was a hit 'n' run. Mum knew she'd killed her but she was running late for Pilates, so she waited till she was back from the gym to move the body and tell us.'

What the *hell* do you say to that?

'Oh . . .' Danielle never makes eye contact so this isn't as awkward as it could be I guess. 'I'll go up and see how Holly's doing.'

When I knock on the bedroom door: 'If it's Paige or Dani, you can come in, but if it's you, Mum, leave me alone, you *murderer*!'

I push the door and find Holly, rolled into a ball of bedding. Nose running. Wow.

I've never had any pets. Oh, okay, I've had *one* pet. A goldfish. Called Sam. He was named after a nurse on *Holby City*. Sadly goldfish Sam died the day after my eighth birthday party. And if I'm perfectly honest, I think that Ollie, the kid from up the road, had something to do with it. I'm not pointing any fingers but he kept asking what fish *felt like*. To be fair to Holly (who is a *mess*) I was devo'd, and being the family drama queen I milked the heartache and mourning process. I drew detailed pictures of Sam. And wrote a short poem to read at his funeral. I resented my brother's fish Slinky (what was *that* name all about?) for the fact that he would outlive Sam. There are photos of the funeral. I'm sporting a *very* wonky fringe and a purple leopard-print belly top. (Just a quick note on belly tops: they were obvs not designed to be worn by kids with actual bellies. However, I spent most of the early noughties dressed like Winnie-the-Pooh.) My five-year-old brother can be seen standing next to me, his eyes closed and hands together in prayer. RIP Sam.

So I do get it, even though I can't fully relate to Holly's pain. I've never been much of a cat person. I sit on the edge of her bed and muster a 'Sorry to hear about Blossom, Hol.'

'Did Danielle tell you that *Mum* did it?!' Her eyes bulge out of her head, all bloodshot and watery.

I nod. She passes me an old photo of Blossom. Like, a printed photograph. Retro. Blossom was old. They'd had her for a long time. Since Holly was about seven.

'She was *my* cat. *I* chose her name,' she sobs. 'She was my best friend. I told her everything.'

I can't help but feel a temporary rush of jealousy towards this dead cat when she says that.

So how do I ask snotty, grieving Holly if she's coming with me to Posers, without sounding like I don't care about dead Blossom and just want to go and draw naked Sue while sitting next to heart-melt gorgeous art school Blaine? Tough one.

'Hol? D'you think getting out of the house might make you feel better?' *Wow, way to go, Paige. Real convincing.*

She sticks out her bottom lip and looks down at the soggy tissue in her hands. 'I'm really pissed off at my mum. I don't want to be here but I can't be arsed to go life drawing now.' Small voice.

Here's the thing – I *desperately* want to go.

'Come on, Hol! *Please*. We're a double act. If you don't come now, it would be like Spongebob going to life drawing without Patrick . . .'

'Which one am I?' She looks at me quizzically.

'You can be Spongebob if you like; I'll be Patrick.' We both laugh at the thought. Gotcha.

She stands to check her reflection in the IKEA mirror. 'I look more like Squidward right now.'

Then she's up, twisting her hair into a bun on top of her head. Trying to cover up her blotchy cheeks with powder and collecting her art materials from the IKEA storage solutions strategically dotted around her room.

Her mum appears at the door. 'Look, Hol, I'm really sorry about Blossom.'

Holly juts her chin up in the air like she's five, as she throws pens and inks into her bag.

'Are you two off out to your class?' She looks at me since Holly's not talking and I confirm that yes, we are. Awk.

'Do you want a lift down there, Hol?'

'Probs best if you don't, Mum. Wouldn't want you to kill Danielle as you reverse out of the garage and leave her to bleed to death until you come home. We'll walk. C'mon, Paige.'

I try *really* hard not to laugh. *Really hard*. But it doesn't work.

On the way to the uni, we go into a corner shop called Happy Times. It's fair to say that those Happy Times have been and gone. It is the saddest shop I've ever seen. We slide the lid on the freezer box and pick out two white-choc Magnums. Outside on the pavement we clink our ice creams together like *Made In Chelsea* champagne glasses.

'To Blossom!'

DRAW ME LIKE ONE OF YOUR FRENCH GIRLS

Clive's here. Still Beige. This must be some kind of *lifestyle choice*. He welcomes us with a wide grin and open arms.

Elspeth is in her corduroy like before and she nods as we pick seats next to her, nearer the front than we were last time. The room is quiet and still.

No sign of Blaine yet. He did say he'd be here. To be fair, he said that just before I chose Bennett's shop floor as the place to declare my undying love to him, so, y'know, it could possibly have scared him away from sitting next to me in Posers for life.

I don't see Sue either. But there's some guy I don't recognise from last week. He's short and round with multiple piercings in and around his face. He's wearing trackie bottoms and a vest. He's stretching by the mattress and avoiding eye contact.

I lean over to Holly and whisper in her ear. 'My money's on him being our Poser for the night.' I wiggle my eyebrows like a pest on a bar stool.

It comes out much louder than I'd anticipated. As per usual. I'm always getting told off for whispering too loud. Or rolling my eyes. Another habit I've tried very hard to kick, but I roll so often that it becomes a physical strain to keep them from doing it.

Poser man looks up at me and says, 'Correctum!'

Did he actually just say *Correctum*? As in rectum? When he's preparing to drop his pants for us to sit around and draw his *actual* arse? Jesus.

Okay, so I won't whisper any more. Like a mind reader, Holly passes me a note on a torn piece of paper from her sketchbook. I unfold it to reveal her accurate observation, scrawled in 6B pencil. 'RECTUM'.

In walks boy-band-handsome Jamie. No hat this time. His hair is longer than I thought it would be. Pushed back off his face, maximising serious boy-band potential. He says a general 'All right' to the room as he takes up a seat behind me and Holly at the back of the room.

I write vintage One Direction lyrics on the back of the Rectum note and pass it to her. I LOL internally. And a tiny bit externally.

Clive's looking at his watch. 'We're still waiting on a few people to turn up so I'm just going to nip out for a fag, amigos.'

There's a bit of laughter and commotion in the corridor and in walks Sue. Fully clothed, sketchbook in hand. She's one of us tonight!

Holly's writing frantically and laughing under her breath. She slips me the paper. 'SUE, I DIDN'T RECOGNISE YOU WITH YOUR CLOTHES ON.'

Sue's the life and soul of the party. She's wearing these kind of dungaree things with paint smeared all over the knees and her wild hair is held up by a metal clip in the shape of a fish.

'All right, Martin, how are you, love?' She sets up an easel as she chats to Correctum, who's doing hamstring stretches like he's about to run a marathon.

I hope Blaine turns up. What if he doesn't? What if I never see him again? Flash forward sixty years and I'll be sitting at a bus stop, stroking an old glove like it's an animal and telling strangers about the boy I never saw again.

'Hello gorgeous, bookshop girls!' Sue winks at us as she unpacks her materials. 'Have you got a petition for me to sign yet?'

I nod, too eager to have her on board. 'Yes we do!'

'Fantastic! Don't leave without showing us the link!'

'We won't let you leave before signing it!' Holly semi-jokes as Sue takes a swig of tea from a huge picnic flask.

I hear voices echoing in the hallway outside, the door swings open and – cue the choral music – it's him. *Dreamy Blaine Henderson.* Laughing with Clive as he strides into the room.

I feel winded when he makes a beeline for the chair next to me and says, 'Good evening, Paige Turner, saviour of the high-street bookshop.'

Before I know it Clive's introducing the class and Correctum is wiggling out of his grey trackies. Oh God. The reality of it hits home; this will be the first naked man I see in *real life*. I blush. Stop the blush. If someone could please invent some kind of anti-blush remedy and Dragon's Den that stuff, it would really help my day-to-day struggle.

He poses with his arms up above his balding head, with his belly and his *genitals* out towards us. No offence to the bloke, there's not much to see. Mostly just belly and tattoos and hair. Like I said, not being at all experienced with boys, or men, the only male nudity references I'm familiar with are *Magic Mike XXL* and the hunky blokes they have on packets on M&S pants. *Irrelevant.*

I'm on the felt-tips today. 'Experimenting with a range of materials' to tick off that criteria box for my coursework. What a loser. I bet *real* artists don't think like that. Bet *Blaine* couldn't care less about getting good marks at college. The true anarchist that he is. *Concentrate on the drawing, Paige. Focus.*

I spend a lot of time detailing the hairs on the chest and the Celtic band Correctum has tattooed round his forearm, but I'm not really sure how to begin tackling his, ahem, *tackle*. So far there's just a blank space above his legs on my drawing. The Most Beautiful Boy In The Universe looks over at my paper and smirks. Does he *know*? Can he tell that I'm totally freaking out about drawing Correctum's shrivelly bits? Oh God, I bet it's so obvious. So blatant that I'm completely clueless. *Look natch, Paige, just go for it.* I do. Get right into it. Think of Sue. Think of Sue. About how it's just like the GCSE wax fruit. *Keep it together, Paige.*

Really, it's just shapes and shadows. And when I think about it like that, rather than crude (anatomically incorrect) genitals scribbled inside hand-me-down French textbooks, it's a *lot* easier to concentrate.

'Thank you.' Clive breaks the silence and asks Correctum for 'another pose when you're ready'. He lies down for this one. Like Rose in *Titanic*, if Kate Winslet was a balding Brummie who liked to make bum jokes.

I get more into drawing and try really hard not to think too hard about *what* I'm drawing, but every now and then I feel feverish when thoughts of sketching the Total Fittie next to me creep into my mind. I bet *Blaine* doesn't have any crappy tattoos like the bloke who's splayed out on the mattress in front of us. I wonder what *his* body looks like. I imagine telling him to '*draw me like one of your French girls*'. How progressive of me. My mind wanders. *Jesus, Paige, keep it together*.

After another pose, which results in a detailed portrait of Correctum's hairy buttocks, it's break time. I look at Holly's work and it's easily one of the most disturbing things I've ever seen. She's drawn cat heads on all of her sketches. Purple Blossom faces instead of Martin heads on every pair of shoulders.

'Wow, Holly. It's . . . Blossom . . .'

'It's my tribute to her. Now she is immortalised in my work.' Her bottom lip wobbles and for a second I'm worried she's ready for Crying Sesh Part Two, until we both burst into laughter.

Boy-band Jamie appears from his seat behind us and pipes up.

'That's sick.' Yes, because in this town people still say 'sick' meaning cool. Does that happen elsewhere? Did it *ever*? I don't know.

'Is it yours?' He raises his eyebrows and points to Holly.

'Erm, yeah.' She steadies her giggles. 'My mum killed my cat today.'

'Mate. That's rough.'

Holly and Jamie look at each other and smile. In my peripheral vision I see The Love Of My Life roll a cigarette and get out of his seat. My heart sinks when he leaves the room.

'Do you go to uni here then?' Holly to Jamie. Smooth.

'Nah. I'm still at college but my mum's a cleaner here. She's never killed any of our pets.' Holly nods and smiles sweetly. Like she's been reading up on flirting tips in the crappy magazines we usually laugh at. It's working, though. He's still talking to her. 'But, yeah, she saw the posters for this and told me. I just get a lift in with her.'

I can actually hear Holly's heart melt like a blue ice pop. I love the blue-flavour ice pops.

Suddenly dying of thirst, and feeling like a third wheel while Holly and Jamie fall madly in love, I wander out of the studio to the vending machine in the corridor.

I press the buttons and watch a bottle of water crash

at the bottom for me to collect.

'Hey.' It's him. Blaine. Coming back along the hallway to class. 'I saw your video by the way.' He means the one Holly made. 'You're pretty much *famous* now. A local celeb.' He teases. 'It's cute.'

I scoff uncontrollably when he says 'cute'. I mean, the video wasn't *meant* to be *cute*. It was meant to be thought-provoking and informative. It's a real issue. Our livelihoods are at stake after all.

But.

If he meant to say he thinks *I'm* 'cute', then . . .

We walk along side by side, and I try not to choke as I sip from my icy water bottle.

'Thanks,' I eventually muster. 'As for being famous . . . I'll try not to let it get to my head.'

He laughs, all floppy hair and cheekbones, and holds the studio door open as I walk in ahead of him.

'And, it's not "cute", by the way.' I narrow my eyes at him and he slumps in his chair.

'Whatever you say, Paige Turner.'

Holly leans on the back of her plastic chair as she recites the petition address to Jamie who punches it into the screen on his phone. That reminds me.

'Here, Sue, can I give you one of these?' I pull a load of

the #SaveBennetts bookmarks from my bag.

'Excellent! Count me in! I'll make everyone I know sign it!'

Clive appears and I pass him a bookmark. 'Hmmmm . . . interesting use of glitter,' he mutters sarcastically. Bit of a bitchy thing for a grown man in his fifties to say if you ask me, but then he adds: 'Wow, yes, we'll help you save Bennett's, of course.' His tone is suddenly more serious once he's read the info. 'Have you put any of these on the noticeboard or in the library? I know it's not as busy here as it is in term time, but it's the degree show next week so this place will fill up . . .'

As Clive gives me beige directions to the campus library and canteen, I try to focus on the conversation without getting completely distracted by the Art School Boy Beauty sitting next to me.

'Thank you. And solidarity!' Clive shoves the bookmark into the back pocket of his trousers and I can't help but feel like all that excess glitter is exactly what his outfit needed. 'Okay then, Posers, take two.'

Correctum is now in some kind of yoga position. I'm pretty sure they call it the tree. I don't even notice that he's naked now; my mind is on other things. On how I *could* just lean over and *touch* Blaine.

Holly slides me a note. I unfold it to read 'COFFEE WITH JAMIE NEXT WEEK – OMGOMGOMG!'

I silently mouth 'Wow' at her. What a smooth operator.

I scribble 'CAN I HAVE SOME OF YOUR MAGIC BOY-CHIRPSING ABILITIES, PLEASE? THANKS. BYE X' and pass it back to her.

She sticks her tongue out in concentration as she jots 'BLAINE TOTES FANCIES YOU BACK!'

My heart skips. Really? Does he *actually* like me *back*?

Then a piece of thicker, heavier paper flies into my lap from the left-hand side. From *HIM*. From Blaine.

I unfold it without looking at him. In scratchy, scribbly writing it says 'PAIGE. HEY. CAN I HAVE MY CHINAGRAPH BACK, PLEASE?'

Oh crap! I look over at him and he's grinning. What do I write back? This is so embarrassing! I kept the pencil at home like some kind of precious artefact! I pretty much STOLE it from him like a crazed super fan! How do I tell him that? I have no idea. I spend seconds agonising over what to say. I fake-rummage for it in my pencil case, knowing it's not in here at all. It doesn't take a critic to know that I wouldn't be winning any Oscars for this terrible performance. I feel his eyes on me expectantly. Okay.

I write 'HEY. I'M SO SORRY. I DON'T KNOW WHERE IT'S GONE! SORRY! I HAVE SOME CHARCOAL, THOUGH?'

Charcoal? Oh, please, we both know that's a poor compromise for the fact I've been hoarding that little piece of him in my room for the past week.

Martin wobbles. He's swaying around. It was an over ambitious pose to be honest. He can't keep his balance on one leg so the other bare foot crashes down onto the dusty mattress. If I was actually drawing now, I'd be pretty *effed off* at that.

I'm not drawing, though.

I'm writing notes to Blaine.

I pass my crappy response to him and open up Holly's note.

Only, oh God, no. It *isn't* Holly's note.

It's the note from Blaine, which means:

I. Gave. Him. Holly's. Note.

No. No. No. No. No.

He's reading 'BLAINE TOTES FANCIES YOU BACK!' I'm looking around the studio for a gun so I can blow my brains out right here, right now.

Oh God. It says 'back'. That's a black-and-white confession that I like him. Now any last *scrappy* chance of playing it cool is long gone.

I take a sideways glance to see that he's tucked the note between the pages at the back of his sketchbook and has gone back to observing Martin.

Thanks a bunch, Martin. Look at what you made me do.

No more notes. Draw. You silly, childish, note-passing idiot. Draw.

Maybe I'll just paint Martin in my own vomit. Since I feel I'd have that material to hand anytime soon. I've never vommed out of *shame* before but, hey, first time for everything.

The rest of the session is a blur. I don't know what's going on.

Why did he just *take* the piece of paper?

Like, could that mean he's okay with me fancying him?

Or maybe he just couldn't bear to look at it. Maybe the thought of a silly little girl like me wanting him is utterly repulsive. Oh God.

After four more wobbly poses from Martin the lesson is over and I rush out of there quicker than I've ever moved in my life.

The Shame.

WINDOW PAIN

Me, Holly and Maxine tiptoe inside the window display.

'It's so dusty in here!' I say, brushing the layer of grey fluff from my black denim knees.

'Be careful not to damage those as you take them down,' Adam warns from his spot behind us on the shop floor.

I smile sweetly, but accidentally-on-purpose tear the NOT NECESSARILY CLOSING-DOWN SALE poster as I pull it out of the display. It feels amazing.

We decided to get rid of these dumb posters and make a new window display. Something that is bright and happy and pulls even more people into supporting the campaign.

I came up with an idea that I'm pretty chuffed with. We've moved the bookcase that was in the staffroom gathering dust into the window. Me and Holly painted big letters that spell out SAVE BENNETT'S onto old cardboard boxes and cut out each individual letter. They're chunky and bright, and we're arranging them on plastic stands and stacks of books on the shelves of the old bookcase. Then we made lots of paper flowers and hearts and stars cut out of old publisher catalogues and free review copies that were piled up in the corner of the staffroom. It's looking even better than it did in my mind.

We also cut out bits of paper that are in the shape of an open book, blank for customers, and us lot, to write reasons for why we want to save Bennett's. We'll stick these to the glass so people passing by can read them. We've made an art installation really. This is hands down much better than any project I've done for Mr Parker at school.

Maxine exhales and pushes her grey fringe back off her lined forehead. 'It's hot in here. I'll step outside to see how it looks.' She's lighting up a cigarette before she's even through the front doors.

Behind a cloud of smoke and on the other side of the glass she nods and gives us a thumbs up, frowning and puffing on her fag.

Holly's phone pings and she smiles, pulling it out of the pocket in the back of her jeans.

'OooOOoooOOh! Is it Jamie again?' I ask, dancing

with excitement, careful not to destroy our bum-kicking window creation.

'Yeah!' I watch her read the screen and immediately tap a reply. Phone back in her pocket. 'I really like him, Paige.'

'And you're so *good* at liking him, Holly! How can you be so cool about it? It's like you have no problem functioning as a Normal Human Being around him, not like me . . .'

'Are you kidding?! I was well nervous chatting to him the other night. I thought it was obvious!'

A group of spotty teenage lads walk past and start gawping at the two of us in the window. It really *must* be a slow day for entertainment in this town.

They shout all manner of politically un-correct insults at us and then one of them kicks an empty plastic Oasis bottle in the direction of the glass and it misses. They're all '*wheeeeeeeeey*'s and tongues and not at all ready for Maxine who's about to go for them.

She glares at one of them and says coolly, 'Give me your phone.'

His cheeks flush and he hands her his iPhone *just like that*.

'Naaaaaah! What did you do that for?!' One of the shorter lads punches his friend on the arm and watches Maxine in disbelief.

Maxine blows smoke rings in the air as she taps on the smartphone screen and pulls up the Save Bennett's petition site.

'Now then, matey boy.' She takes a drag. 'You and the cast of *The Inbetweeners* here are going to enter your name and email addresses on this site, okay? You're going to do me and these girls a favour by saving our jobs, and you're going to do yourselves a favour by paying us a visit – once you've calmed down – so you can attempt to *read a bloody book*.' She blows smoke into his Clearasil face and smiles. 'Okay?'

Without even having to look at Holly, I *know* that her face is pressed up against the glass just like mine is. To our astonishment the other boys actually stop and get their phones out.

One of them winks at me and I really want to make it clear that I'm not at all interested, but I'm too busy standing here with a pair of rusty scissors, in *awe* of Maxine's Bad Gal Attitude.

She throws her fag on the pavement and stubs it out under her vegan leather ankle boot, before walking back into the shop and climbing back into the window as though she hadn't just blown our tiny impressionable minds.

STOP THE PRESS

My eyes sting at the laptop screen as I sit on the edge of my bed in my pants.

I was getting dressed, until I got completely wrapped up in an iPlayer documentary presented by Reggie Yates. He's in Uganda.

A tatty van with a faded paint job that reads MOBILE LIBRARY pulls up along a dusty road and suddenly hundreds of children run towards it. They smile and skip and dance with books clutched to their hearts. Books with damaged spines and dog-eared corners. They're so excited to borrow these books and to read.

How can we, here in *Greysworth*, say that we've had enough of bookshops, of libraries, of *access to books*? That they're outdated and irrelevant. Unimportant. While there are children in parts of this world *running* towards *books*, how can we possibly say 'Enough. It's time to get rid of bookshops; it's time to clear them from our high streets'?

'Paaaaaaige!' Mum calls from downstairs. She's back from her early-morning trip to town. I pull a spotty sundress over my head and shut my laptop, silencing Reggie Yates as he asks a small boy what his favourite thing about school is.

In the kitchen, Elliot spoons chocolate-flavoured cereal into his mouth and Mum holds a copy of the local newspaper. 'Look what I picked up on my way to the jobcentre!'

'OMG! Did they print it? Can I see?!'

She dances around on the kitchen tiles before turning to the article that covers the Save Bennett's story.

I beam. 'Yep, that's us! Right between the *shocking* news that the 99p Store is about to reopen as a Poundland and . . . Oh! The fascinating story about a *hat* that has been found up a tree!'

As much as the *Chronicle* is a bit of a joke, it's good to get some campaign coverage in here. They've included a link to the petition site and there's a photo of us in front of the new window display. I look like a right geek, grinning away at the camera. Holly is obviously trying to look pretty, and it works: one hand on her hip as she pouts, like it was taken right before a big night out. Maxine looks ferocious, evidently using the time it took to take the photo as a fag break. Adam has his eyes shut. Tony has his usual look of bewilderment and disgust on his face. We make a motley crew.

This shot was taken just *seconds* before Tony got drenched in seagull poo. The obscenities that came out of his mouth at that would earn the film adaptation of my life an 18 certificate. I'm pretty sure he terrified the timid reporter who had been sent out by the *Chronicle*. Her name was Alison Weaver. She had sensible shoes and hair the colour of apricot Petits Filous. I held her big shiny camera while she fumbled around on her phone and signed the petition.

Back in the kitchen. 'Can you fetch me some scissors, El?'

'Um, *no*. Get them yourself.'

After thirteen years of having a younger brother, I still find it hard to accept the fact that he won't be my pet slave.

'Eugh, *fine*.'

As Mum tells us about her most recent 'farcical' trip to the jobcentre, I snip our story out of the paper, so I can Blu-Tack it to the wall in my room.

'Well done, Paigey!' Mum puts her arm round my

shoulders. 'I'm really proud of you for getting this far.'

'Yeah, well done, *Paigey*.' Elliot smirks. 'Shame they couldn't get a photo of you where you didn't look like a *total circus freak . . .*'

'Oi!'

I take a photo of the article and post it all over the blog, the Bennett's Twitter page, my Instagram and Facebook profiles. I hashtag for eternity.

I dial Holly's number on my phone. Wait for her to pick up. She has a habit of changing her ringtone to her fave songs. I know for a fact that she delays answering, just so she can get through most of the song before it gets to voicemail. I picture her dancing along to whatever she's set it as now and it makes me laugh.

'Holly! Have you seen the paper? We're in it!'

'OMG! Yes I just saw it on Facey B. Of course, it's not the *first* time I've been papped by *The Chron . . .*'

It's true. When Holly was in Year Two she won a competition to design an anti-dog-fouling poster at school. Her entry was used on signs in Abington Park and there's a clipping in her house of a very proud eight-year-old Holly holding a felt-tip depiction of a crying turd. Her two front teeth are missing, and it's the perfect balance of hilarious and adorable. The kind of pic they dig up from your past when you're a celeb, making an appearance on a chat show with a cheeky host who wants to embarrass you. Holly will never be embarrassed by that story; she tells it to most people within seconds of meeting them.

'Are you ready to roll if I leave my house now?' I ask.

'Yes! See you ASAP!'

I shove my feet into the already laced-up Doc Martens near the front door. 'Okay, Mum, I'm on my way out. Me and Holly are meeting Sue from Posers. She's going to help us print some campaign slogan T-shirts.'

'Have fun! Hope you're not hounded by the press now that you're a local news story! And for God's sake make sure you're wearing knickers if you get papped getting in or out of any flashy cars!'

'If it was guaranteed to get us a thousand signatures on the petition then I wouldn't wear any!' I lie.

I wouldn't *actually* do that by the way.

CIVIL DISOBEDIENCE

Sue flicks a switch on the radio and Heart FM echoes around the walls of the print room.

'Thanks for agreeing to do this, Sue. Hope you didn't mind us using your email address from the petition site to contact you.'

'Not at all! I'm so happy that I can help in some way.' She prises the lid off a tin of black ink.

It occurred to me that we should have SAVE BENNETT'S T-shirts. All the good campaigns I've been obsessing over online seem to have slogan tees and I asked Holly and Adam if they thought it was a good idea. Lucky they did because I'd already placed a bid on a job lot of plain white tees from eBay.

'Right then, girls, gather round.' The two of us stand in paint-splattered aprons on either side of Sue, as she shows us how to screen-print.

She leans over the table and pulls the squeegee in towards her chest, pushing a thin layer of paint through the stencil. 'You've got to move fast and really put your back into it.'

We watch in awe as she lifts the screen to reveal our very first SAVE BENNETT'S T-shirt.

'That's so cool!' I gush and she stands back with her hands on her hips like *I told you so*.

'Right, your turn. Now lay a fresh T-shirt underneath. Make sure it's completely flat.'

The campus security guard hovers by the door.

Sue pretends to take over with the printing until he walks on.

'I'm not *really* supposed to let you in here . . .' she confesses as I pull the paint over the stencil. 'You're *supposed* to have had an official induction to the print room, but oh well!' She grimaces. 'Think of it as civil disobedience.'

'Um . . . what's civil disobedience?' Holly asks, looking slightly embarrassed. I'm glad she asked, and I'm glad I'm not the only one who's never heard of it.

'It's the refusal to comply with certain laws, as a peaceful form of political protest. It's breaking the rules, without *really* doing anything "bad".'

I lift up the screen, chuffed with my rebellious creation and at the idea of peaceful political protest.

Back at Holly's house, she places her beloved first volume of the I'm a Murderer trilogy in my hands.

She catches me wrinkling my nose at it. I'm not at all into gruesome, kill-y crime thrillers like she is.

'Please just give it a go, Paige. I promise you'll be hooked.'

'Okaaaaay . . .' I do my best to sound enthusiastic, turning the chunky thing over on my lap to skim-read the blurb.

'I *need* someone else to read it so we can discuss it together. At length.'

'Paula Williamson,' I read the author's name out loud.

'Ohmygod she's a genius. I hope she appreciates that if Bennett's closes, it's not only the town of Greysworth that'll be suffering; it's me! It's my mental well-being! I *neeeeeed* to get my hands on the final part of this series when it comes out. Fat chance we'll get it in at the school library. Far too violent.'

I open my mouth to remind her for the millionth time that it's just not my kind of thing, but then Holly declares that it's time for a photo shoot. Costume change! She spills over the cups of her bra as she finds the armholes in her T-shirt. Then she ties a knot at the front, cropping it slightly so that it obscures the logo but shows off her pillowy belly. She lays every gold-plated chain she owns from Claire's round her neck for some activist-babe bling.

I roll the sleeves up on mine, so it's not quite as baggy on my pink arms. Holly provides a selfie stick, extending it dramatically like it's a deadly weapon. Selfie Samurai Princess. She snaps us modelling our home-made, rule-breaking protest T-shirts and uploads it onto the blog.

A MILLION TINY PAPERCUTS

'Holly!' I call her name as she dumps a heavy bag for life of shopping in the boot of her mum's car.

'Hey, Paige! What are you doing here?' She frown-laughs, like it's *not* normal to be hanging around the car park behind Morrison's.

'Well, I called your house earlier and Danielle told me you were here –' I unfold the spare SAVE BENNETT'S T-shirt I brought along for her – 'and seeing as we are *so* near our thousand-signature target, I was thinking that we should hit the high street. Ask people to sign up face to face. A final push to get our numbers up.' I jump onto the kerb and sing, 'Are you with me?!'

'What, now? Today, you mean?'

'Um, yeah?' What's her problem? 'We need to hit that target, Holly. Remember what the Make a Change website said, about waiting *five working days* for a response from the council? Well, it's Monday already, so we only have a week until the shop is due to close! We're only one hundred signatures away from *not* screwing this up!'

I wait for Holly to react to my plan of action, but she just blinks at me.

'Look!' I offer, opening the pink folder I've cleverly labelled ACTIVISM SHIZ. 'We just collect the same info from them on paper. Name, email address and signature . . .'

I see her mum sitting in the driver's seat of the car as she watches our convo in the rear-view mirror.

'But I can't this afternoon, *remember*? I'm meeting Jamie for coffee.'

It's not that I'd *forgotten* she was going out with Jamie; after all, I've been privy to some in-depth discussions about what she should wear to their date. I *did* kind of forget that it was happening *today*, though. It really isn't a good time.

'Well, okay, where are you meeting him? Can't you just help me out with this beforehand?'

'Paige.' She rests her hand on my shoulder, and looks me square in the eyes, like I'm thick or something. I know she's just trying to reason with me but that doesn't make it any less irritating. 'I'm meeting Jamie at the cafe in the park, and

I have to go home and get ready before then. Food shopping is sweaty work! I need a shower, babe! Have you *seen* the state of my hair?!' She snorts.

The cafe in the park is *miles* away from town, so there's no way she's going to be able to help me with this. I kick at the car park gravel and like a mind reader, Holly starts justifying her decision to meet him at the place where 'You *know* they do the best iced latte! And! *And* I'll show Jamie the albino peacock in the mini aviary.'

'The albino peacock's *name* is Lord Sparkle the Third.' I pout. Disappointed that I'll be here in town, Billy No Mates (and No Comrades Supporting The Cause), while Holly and Jamie enjoy a perfect day at the park with the world's freakiest bird.

Okay, Jamie seems like a nice guy.

Okay, he's so good-looking that it's as if he has a permanent Instagram filter over his body.

But –

'I just can't believe you're breaking the Girl Code for some guy. That's all.' It comes out a lot whinier than I'd intended.

She scowls at me. 'What? You expect me to drop everything because you've suddenly had an idea? No, Paige. I already have plans and you *knew* that.'

'Eugh, fine. Whatever.'

It's not fine. I can't believe she's picking a boy over the campaign. Over *me*.

I walk away. I can't be bothered with this. I've got bigger fish to fry.

Bigger, vegetarian, metaphorical fish to fry.

'Paige!' she calls after me. 'There's no need to be such a *bitch* about it.'

It slices through me like a million tiny paper cuts. I stop in my tracks. 'Oh my God! As *if* you just called me a bitch! Y'know what, Holly? I hope you *choke* on your poxy iced latte!'

I storm through the market square fuming at Holly. The same old market where we paid over the odds for salty chips on rainy Saturday afternoons, huddled together by the warmth of the van. I push past rails and rails of granny knickers and nighties, past the blokes who sit surrounded by neon signs offering to UNLOCK PHONES HERE.

I mutter every single nasty thing I can think about her to no one in particular.

Eventually I end up at the door to Coleman's Stationery Suppliers. If I'm going to do this alone, then I need a clipboard. To get people to support the cause and give me their details, I should look more official than I do right now: a sixteen-year-old loser with a wonky fringe who's just been dumped by her best friend.

PiNCH ME!

Coleman's has one of those old-fashioned doors that rings as you push it open.

For a stationery addict like me, this place is an Aladdin's cave. This place is the reason I've never dreaded the first day of term because it means new supplies and freshly sharpened pencils, which is enough to make me swoon. It's pokey and quiet and the shelves are stacked so high that you can't see over the top or round corners. It's like you're in a maze of Post-it notes and Pritt Sticks. Like one of those hedge mazes they have in stately homes on school trips. Like the one in *The Shining*. Well, kind of like the one in *The Shining*, without the snow, or the creepy kid, or the psychotic murderer (hopefully).

I take my time finding my way through the aisles,

constantly side-tracked by sketchbooks and highlighters and raffle ticket books (seriously, even raffle ticket books). They have *everything* here.

Sharpeners. Fine liners. Novelty-shaped erasers. Label-makers. I desperately want a label-maker. How tragic is that? Pencil cases. You can never have too many pencil cases. I'm investigating a fluffy puppy-shaped zip-up when suddenly, somebody behind me says: 'Paige.'

Still clutching the pencil case, I turn round to see where that came from. As I do, my bag knocks a plastic jar of jumbo drawing pins all over the burgundy carpet. They scatter like confetti and before I can even bend to pick them up–

Oh Em Gee, it's Blaine.

He's down on the floor, clearing up the mess I've made.

I'm so shocked to see him here that I'm squeezing the life out of this puppy pencil case. Even George from *Of Mice and Men* would be like, 'Time out, Paige. Put the poor creature down.'

'I'm sorry! I just – You made me jump. Let me help.' I kneel and collect a handful of prickly pins from the ground.

'This is what I have to put up with: bookshop girls turning up and trashing the place.' He's cocky as. He smirks at me, his face *centimetres* from mine, and the tiny hoop earring he has through his ear shines in the florescent strip lights. It's glorious.

I feel like I have some kind of Looney-Toons-style jaw-drop going on right now, as he stands up straight. So tall. So, so, tall.

'I had no idea you worked here,' I confess, jumping to my feet and feeling the blood rush to my head. I relish the opportunity to appreciate his uniform.

I have never seen an uglier uniform worn by such a beautiful human being. He is working it. Who *knew* a red polyester waistcoat could look so fit? He's wearing a hideous tie with a paperclip pattern on it, and somehow he looks more handsome than ever. I flashback to the last time I saw him, when I made that fatal note-passing blunder at Posers, and shake it away, out of my mind.

'Yeah. I work here. Part-time. Fit it around my course . . . So, how can I help?'

'Oh . . .' I try to remember exactly what it is I'm doing here. 'Clipboards! I need a clipboard. Do you have those?'

'Right this way . . .' I follow him closely through aisles tightly packed with squared paper and gel pens and staplers. 'What do you need a clipboard for anyway?' He leans on a metal shelf, giving me space to check out the extensive selection of stationery on offer.

'Oh, well, it's for the petition actually. We need more signatures, and we need to get them by tomorrow. So, I'm hitting the high street!' I fall silent when I think of Holly.

'What's wrong?' Blaine asks.

'Well, I wanted my best friend, Holly, to help me with it, but –' *she thinks I'm a bitch and she told me so* '– but, she's busy, so I'm doing this alone.'

'Oh? Do you want a hand?' He shrugs. 'I finish my shift in, like, fifteen minutes, so if you want someone to help, I'd be up for it.'

OMG! This is a staff announcement: please could a cleaner report to the clipboard aisle? There has been a serious spillage. A major Crush Gush.

Yes. Oh God, yes. One million times, YES!

'Cool. That would be great.' The *ma-hoo-siv-est* understatement of the century.

When I count out my change for the clipboard, it's a bit awks because I'm 50p short.

Crap. I rummage at the bottom of my bag in search of coins, desperate not to let the super-absorbent Bodyform pad flop out and on to the counter.

'Don't worry about it.' He puts my money in the till and says, 'It's only fifty p.'

I guess Coleman's is a pretty laid-back place to work;

there's no way I'd get away with discrepancies like that at Bennett's.

'I'll meet you outside when I finish. Wait for me out there, yeah?'

I skip out of the shop, nearly tripping over my happy feet and try so hard to look casual once I'm on the pavement outside.

Discreetly pinching at my wrist for a reality check, I, Paige Turner, am waiting for *Blaine Henderson* to meet me.

EVEN SWEETER THAN PINK STARBURSTS

He wouldn't be here if he didn't like you. If he was really repulsed by the note you passed him at life drawing, then he wouldn't choose to spend time with you right now.

'Let's start here,' I suggest, attaching the home-made sign-up sheets to my brand-new, *official* clipboard. That familiar smell of market-square fried onions hangs over us.

'Sure.' I try to avoid staring directly at Blaine, but I defo catch him checking his reflection in the window of Costa. He plays with the dark floppy mass of hair on top of his head and exudes Sulky Arty Boy sex appeal. He's replaced his polyester waistcoat with a leather jacket. I mean, jeez, if I was him, I'd check myself out in every reflective surface too.

It's busy around here this afternoon, and I'm determined to approach everybody we see. Quite a lot of people mistake us for charity workers, and do all they can to avoid being spoken to, suspicious that it might mean parting with their cash. But once we get chatting to the market traders, the support begins to show.

I thought I'd be the one doing most of the talking, but when it comes to telling people about the campaign Blaine is so passionate about fighting The Cause. He expresses himself with clenched fists when describing The Injustice of Losing Bennett's to 'The Man'. I wonder if this is for my benefit. Y'know, if these monologues and rhetorical questions are supposed to impress me. It's working. I am impressed. He is so dreamy.

I think we make a good team.

The clock outside the shopping centre strikes. We've already been out here for an hour and a half. One of the sign-up sheets is already filled with the names and emails of new Bennett's supporters. We're halfway there. Just another hour or so until it'll die down here; I reckon we'll be able to collect another fifty signatures.

'Thanks. For helping me, I mean. I think we've done really well.'

I'm massively playing my excitement down for the sake of seeming cool. I'm thrilled that we've got all these new names on the list of supporters. I'm overjoyed that the boy I fancy is here helping me do this.

As I rummage in my bag for my ACTIVISM SHIZ folder, Blaine clocks the SAVE BENNETT'S T-shirt I brought along for Holly. 'Is that a spare?'

'Oh, yeah. We made a whole run of them with Sue from Posers.'

'Can I have it?'

Duh! Of course you can have it. Have everything. Take it all.

This is all happening so fast. I chuck him the tee. He shrugs out of his jacket and passes it to me. 'Hold this for me?'

I'm holding his leather jacket in my hands.

Oh God. He's unbuttoning his shirt. Right here. In front of me. In the market square.

'Oi! Are you perving on me, Paige Turner?'

'No!' I lie, my eyeballs suddenly glued to the fascinating cobbles beneath my feet.

He stretches the T-shirt over his chest and ruffles his hair back into place.

'How do I look?'

Delicious.

'Yeah. Great. Cool. Okay.'

'SUPPORT YOUR LOCAL BOOKSHOP!' He grabs

the attention of yet another group of old ladies, who immediately fall for his charms.

While a road sweeper in a high-vis jacket adds his signature to our ever-growing list, Blaine leans in close and says, 'I'll be back in a sec – going to buy some fags.'

I watch the tank of blue and red ice swirl around in the Slush Puppie machine while I wait for him to reappear from inside the corner shop. Bobby the Busker plays an atrocious rendition of a barely recognisable song. The sun is shining, and an audience of locals gather round to clap along (out of time).

'I got you these.' Blaine hands me a packet of Starburst. Just like that. Just like he *knows* chewy, fruity sweets are my faves and that plying me with them means I'll love him forevs, no matter what.

'Oh, wow, thanks!' Unstoppable Cheshire Cat grin right now. 'Do you want one?' I offer, tearing at the outer wrapper.

'Nah. I'm sweet enough.' He air-kisses me and I die.

The first sweet in the packet is pink. Pink! My favourite flavour!

Could this day actually get any better?!

As Blaine tucks an unlit cigarette behind his ear, and

pulls me by the hand, I'm certain that, yes, this day is about to get even better.

'What are you doing?!' I squeal, too excited by this skin-to-skin contact.

'Dance with me!' I drop my bag and the clipboard on the pavement and follow him to the cobbles. He laces his fingers between mine and sings along to Bobby the Busker. I can't stop laughing. Fried onions in the air and the taste of strawberry Starburst on my tongue.

It all seems too good to be true. I'd seriously consider this all being a dream, but if it was one of my dreams, something freaky would have happened by now. Like that one where my whole body was covered in ingrown hairs.

An even larger crowd gathers round to watch us and Blaine plays up to it. He pouts and shimmies and he even twirls me, like this is some low-budget Disney flick. I spin and spin and when I snap back to face him we are close. So close. I don't think I'm moving any more. But I do think that his eyes are on my lips, and I wonder if my lips look as dry as they feel right now.

I wonder if – Is he going to . . . *kiss me*, right here? In the market square? As we dance to Bobby the Busker?

'OI!' The old bloke in the mobility scooter shatters my Blaine-Snogging Dream World to pieces. 'THIEF!'

It takes a split second for me to catch up. Two lads rip past us on a push bike. The one on the back clutches *my bag* in his hands.

'That's *mine*!' I cry.

Why did I leave it there on the pavement?! How could I be so *stupid*?

'OI!' Blaine roars and sprints after them. 'Get back here!'

I chase behind, as fast as I can, a stitch already slowing me down.

It almost happens in slow motion. Blaine catches up with them and the lads topple off the bike. Just as he grabs one of them by the collar, I see the other guy take my phone and chuck my bag and the rest of its contents into the fountain on the high street.

No.

No.

No.

They scramble back onto the bike and speed into the distance and Blaine howls expletives at them until they vanish.

I crash into the side of the concrete water feature, where sanitary towels and spare hair ties bob along on the murky water. I whimper as I watch the sheets of petition signatures floating across the surface. Completely ruined.

SILLY COW

I scrunch my face into my pillow, which is already soaked by all the snot and tears.

Yeah, it's embarrassing, but I cried pretty much the whole way back. Like *that* little piggy. *Wee wee wee all the way home.*

I didn't make any attempt to dry myself when I got in and now I'm lying here shivering.

Phoneless.

Friendless.

And pretty much jobless.

It started raining as I trudged home. It wasn't even just a little shower, but huge biblical raindrops. How ridiculous and dramatic. Miss Tomlinson told us one English lesson that it's called 'pathetic fallacy' when the weather reflects a mood. She's right about the 'pathetic' bit. That's exactly how I felt, trudging home in the downpour, puddles in my soggy shoes.

What was I *thinking* leaving my bag and the petition right there on the ground? So wrapped up in making an utter prat of myself, dancing with Blaine, that I let that come before the campaign?

If I hadn't been the living, breathing, human answer to the emoji with heart eyes, then I wouldn't have screwed everything up.

Blaine didn't want to get his hair wet, so I ended up climbing into the fountain and fishing out my belongings.

By the time I picked the clipboard and sign-up sheets out of the water, they were beyond repair. On the pieces of paper that were still intact, the ink had bled and was illegible.

A couple of community support police officers with noisy walkie-talkies wandered by. They told me to get out of the fountain and said someone had seen Blaine punch a boy on a bike.

I didn't stick around to tell them what had happened; it was too late to change anything. I didn't say goodbye to Blaine either. I was too embarrassed and upset and wet.

Now it's dark, it's pouring with rain, and there's no

way I'm going to be able to collect a hundred signatures before tomorrow.

It's over. Thanks to me.

I wish I could go back in time to the moment I thought I could help or change any part of this hopeless situation. I wish I could go back to that point and tell myself to shut up, that I'm in no fit state to save the last bastion of a dying trade.

I curl into a ball and pull the duvet cover round my wet shoulders. If only I could make myself really small.

Make myself tiny. Tiny enough to live comfortably inside the Sylvanian Families Treehouse Nursery, which I can see gathering dust on top of my wardrobe. I'd like to sit on the tiny plastic chair. Play a tune on the miniature piano. Eat Sylvanian-scale baguettes from the Sylvanian Bakery. I bet everything's fan-*bloody*-tabulous in Sylvania. I bet there aren't any Sylvanian phone thieves, chucking Sylvanian hopes and dreams into the Sylvanian fountain.

Eugh.

Look at this place. Who do I even think I *am* trying to lead a revolution when my room is like some weird museum of childhood memorabilia that's been attacked by a bra-flinging, hairspray-can hoarding . . . *loser*?

Downstairs Mum watches the telly. She's a hundred per

cent with me when it comes to thinking I'm the Silliest Cow for wrecking the petition for the sake of dancing with a boy. The local news is on and the headline about a cow getting its head stuck in a plastic chair muffles through the walls. '*It is not yet known how the chair or the cow came to be in the field . . .*'

I groan in despair.

Usually I'd call Holly.

But after this morning's fall-out what am I supposed to tell her? After guilt-tripping her for not helping me, and then royally *effing* it up myself.

That book she lent me is here, right next to my bed. *I'm a Murderer* by Paula Williamson.

I open it for the first time, blinking through my watery eyes.

Wow. Holly's annotated the entire book. She's actually written her own notes in the margins. She's circled and underlined bits, and even drawn love hearts next to 'fave victims'. I can't help but laugh. This is such a weird thing to do. It's such a Holly thing to do.

Right at the front, she's scrawled her own theories as to who the murderer is. I can just about make out the name of the publisher beneath her loopy handwriting. It says their offices are based in London.

I open my laptop and start writing an email that I'm ninety-nine per cent sure I have zero intention of ever sending. I tap away at the keyboard so furiously that I make millions of typos and stop even feeling like this is a real email to a real person.

For the attention of bestselling author Paula Williamson,

Don't worry. Obvs I'm not COMPLETELY deluded – I know that you'll never read this. I'm not actually going to send it and even if I did, you're so busy writing books my bessie's obsessed with that I doubt you'll ever get a chance to read about the fall-out we had today and how she called me a bitch and I danced with Blaine (who's really fit but really bad at fetching precious data out of crappy water features) and how I've ruined EVERYTHING FOR EVERYBODY. BLEUGH!

It's all a mess. A huge mess.

My name is Paige and I work in a bookshop called Bennett's, in a town called Greysworth. Recently we were told that we'd have to close down because we wouldn't be able to afford the rent, and obviously this is heartbreaking because Bennett's is the single best thing about being born and having to exist in Greysworth. We tried really hard to save Bennett's. We made a petition and were doing pretty well until I managed to cock that up too. Now it's too late and it looks like we'll be closing for good. Which sucks. Because there's nothing else to do around here.

My best friend Holly is such a huge fan of your I'm a Murderer *books that she writes her own theories in the margins and she can't bear the thought of not being a bookshop girl when the third and final part of the series is published at the end of the year.*

Anyway. She'd be made up (and hopefully maybe) forgive me if she realised that you'd known about Bennett's. If you'd known that she was there, in Greysworth, promoting your stories and sharing her love for them to anyone with ears.

Okay, well, thanks I guess and LOL.

Paige Turner X

Bennett's, Greysworth

Without rereading it I click send.

Piss it.

There's nothing to lose.

As I retreat back into my heap of bedding, the house

phone rings and I hear my brother answer it.

Now Elliot is knocking on my door. My door. The six-foot collage of Barbie and Teletubby stickers that survived two and a half 'I'm grown up and over this' peel-off attempts.

He offers me the phone but I silently shake my head.

Holding it back to his ear, Elliot lies, 'She can't talk right now. Ah, okay. Yeah, right. All right, yeah. I'll tell her, yeah . . .' He absently picks at a faded Pokémon sticker. As long as it's not the Jigglypuff one I'll let it slide. 'Okay. Yeah . . . Okay, will do. It's Holly.'

I hope she's not still angry at me.

She will be if I blow her off now.

I take the phone from my brother and mumble something tiny along the lines of 'Helloholly . . .'

'Paige! Ohmygod! I want to hear *all about* your day in town, but before I do I just want to apologise for earlier. I'm *so*, *so*, sorry –'

She's speaking so fast that I reckon she's downed every iced latte within a five-mile radius of Greysworth.

'– and I just wanted to let you know that while we were at the park today, me and Jamie collected a *load* of signatures for the campaign! Think we've got well over a hundred! There was some kind of lame concert on at the band stand, so the place was packed!'

'Oh, Holly!' I wail. 'That's amazing!' I'm defs going to cry again. 'You beauty! You absolute legend! You've saved the day!' I could do the Macarena for eternity, I am that proud.

I dissolve into tears of joy, jump around my silly, childish, happy room and physically kiss the phone with relief.

'Now, before I tell you about the surreal day I had in town with *Blaine Henderson* –' I hear her gasp on the other end of the line – 'I want to hear *every single detail* about your date with Jamie.'

DIRECT ACTION

I arrived late to Posers this evening.

Uploading the signatures Holly and Jamie collected on to the petition site took forever, and then submitting the thing took even longer.

Sue was already splayed across the mattress when I stumbled into the studio and as soon as I noticed that Jamie had pinched my usual spot next to Holly, I had to awkwardly scrape a spare chair into position. Real subtle.

Now I'm *still* out of breath, desperately trying to catch up with the rest of the class by sketching the curve of Sue's fleshy back.

'Great. Thank you, Sue; you can relax now.' Clive sets his graphite stick down on the ledge of his easel. 'Let's take that tea break, shall we, gang?'

Break time already? Guess I was even later than I thought.

Blaine stretches out of his chair. 'I see you've dried off since your paddle in the fountain . . .'

'It's not funny!' I plead.

God, last time I saw him I was a total wreck, crying like a baby as I fished my Bodyform pads and broken dreams out of the water. 'I'm sorry I left in such a hurry . . .' I explain. 'Did you get in trouble with those police officers?'

'Pfffft! Nah, "pigs" don't scare me. I'm not worried about them. They're just puppets. Part of a machine.' He snarls, places an unlit cigarette between his lips and winks, before swaggering out of the studio. His secondhand brogues tap along the paint-splattered floor.

Still swooning, I turn to Holly who is giving the back of Blaine's leather jacket some seriously filthy looks.

'What's wrong?' I ask.

'I still think it *sucks* that he basically *threw* your stuff in the fountain and that *you're* the one who ended up getting in there to get it back . . .'

'He didn't *throw* it in there, Hols. The lads on the bike –'

'Well, *pretty much*.' She narrows her eyes and taps her pencil on her sketchbook disapprovingly. 'I'm not sure about that Blaine Henderson. I don't trust him.'

Jamie joins in, laughing under his breath. 'I know what you mean. He seems a bit pretentious, doesn't he? He loves himself a bit too much.'

OMG! I really don't appreciate Holly bringing this up in front of Jamie. Since when did he become the invisible third member of our gruesome twosome?!

Sue pads over to us, robe on. 'So what's the latest from our splinter group of bookshop activists?'

'We've submitted the petition!' I cheer, remembering that, as much as the lovebirds sitting here have hurt me by slating Blaine, they *are* responsible for saving the petition, and saving me from suffocating in my snotty, tear-stained duvet cover.

'Fan-tas-tic!' Sue claps her hands together. 'It's a waiting game now.'

Waiting is not my strong point. I've spent a lifetime rattling presents under Christmas trees and Googling plot spoilers to my favourite TV shows.

'Don't leave it too long, though,' Sue warns, tidying the wild strands of hair that fall into her eyes. 'Direct action. That's what needs to happen. If they won't pay attention to everything you've done so far, you need to do something, a campaign stunt, that they will have no choice but to sit up and pay attention to. If your petition doesn't get the message across, then it's time to take a more forceful approach.'

'No more Mr Nice Guy!' says Holly, laughing and totally getting onto Sue's wavelength.

'You can still be civil, peaceful . . .' Sue clarifies. 'You mustn't forget your principles. Taking direct action is the next step. It's giving civil disobedience a bit of welly!'

Blaine and Clive breeze through the door in a cloud of smokers' coughs.

'Right, let's get back into it, Posers! Sue, what do you fancy? A long or a short pose next?'

I'm making marks on my paper. Marks that kind of resemble Sue. Evidence that I'm drawing, but I'm not on Sue at all. My mind is on anything *but* Sue.

How could Holly and Jamie think that Blaine is pretentious?! Untrustworthy?!

They probably just don't *get* him.

He's not really like the other lads around this town.

He reads all the books I want to read when I'm at work.

He's arty, and intellectual, and he's an *anarchist*.

He's perfect for me. I'm pretty sure we're meant to be together, so Holly and Jamie will just have to get used to it.

While I steal glances at Blaine throughout the class,

those two words, 'direct action', are dancing around my head like two drunken aunties at a wedding.

Direct action.

Of course.

OPEN LETTER

I squint at the cracked screen on Holly's phone while we stand behind the till. The campaign video she uploaded last week has had hundreds of hits, and comments are still rolling in: people offering their support, wishing us well.

'I hate waiting around to hear back from the council,' I moan. The fact that the urgency of our situation doesn't seem to be being taken seriously is really grating on me.

'Did Take That teach you nothing, Paige?' Adam jests. 'You're lacking in what Gary Barlow would refer to as "a little patienc—"'

'*Take That? Gary Barlow?*' I frown. 'What are you talking about?'

He shakes his head and says something about forgetting 'how *young*' me are Holly are before continuing. 'It's only been two days since we submitted the petition. The guidelines did say that it could take as long as five working days to get a response . . .'

'Time's running out, though!' I tap at the imaginary watch on my wrist. This is our last week of trading according to the notice period that Mick Morgan from head office gave us just over three weeks ago.

It's making me anxious.

After what Sue said about direct action, I can't help but feel like rather than waiting for an answer, twiddling our thumbs, we need to try something else.

'Okay so, guys, I've drafted an open letter.' I open the notebook I started scrawling in this morning when Mr Abbott approaches the desk, pink cherryade stain on his white moustache.

'Any new books on pig farming?'

We have already explained to him that no new books are being delivered at the moment, but he's not getting it.

'Sorry, Mr Abbott. We don't have any new pig books.' I smile and try to be as polite as possible, even though I know how long this could go on for, and I know exactly what line's coming next.

'I think I know a bit more about pigs than you do!' That glimmer in his pale eyes as he smiles.

'Yes, yes, I imagine you do.'

He sighs and stands propped up by his walking stick. A heavy, quilted Barbour jacket is wrapped round him, despite it being one of the hottest days of the year.

We watch him shuffle over to his seat by the window and Holly asks, 'What *is* a, a what? An open letter?'

'Oh, yeah, so I've seen a few of them on my online travels into activism now . . . and basically what I've gathered is that it's a letter addressed directly to the person you've got beef with . . .'

Holly snorts. '*Beef!* Like Shayleigh and Charlotte Evans!'

Of course. Throwback to Year Eight when two girls in our class organised a huge fight by the shops because Shayleigh had accused Charlotte of texting her boyfriend.

'OMG yes! Exactly like that! So, like, remember how Charlotte Evans wrote that long post on Facebook about how she had beef with Shayleigh?'

'*Like I'd ever link your boyfriend he's so crusty!*' Holly does an outstanding impression of our classmate that makes me *wish* our CCTV was in operation so that I could relive it again and again.

'And in that status, Charlotte addressed Shayleigh, and she wrote down exactly what her *beef* was and what she was going to do about it, but we could all read it so we all knew what was going on; that's kind of like an open letter!'

'Brilliant!' She claps her hands in excitement.

'So, I was thinking, if we write an open letter to the council and we tell them about the petition, and the support we've gained so far, and that it would be a *humungous* loss to the high street if they let the plans for demolition to go ahead . . .'

'Yes yes yes!'

'Then we post it online, on our blog, and we share it, and we get other people to share it, and the fact that so many people have read this letter, puts extra pressure on the council to act on it . . .'

Adam nods and strokes his beard. 'I mean, it's not like the council *own* Bennett's or these premises but . . . they do have the power and the authority to challenge plans to demolish us . . .'

'Exactly! They also have a responsibility to communicate the fact that the people of this town *do* want a bookshop on their high street. We've got the petition to prove it.' I beam with pride. 'On top of that, they must be aware of the number of jobs that will be lost if we close, and the fact that we'd be *another* shop pushed out of the centre because of "high-street regeneration", which so far only seems to push businesses out of town when they can't afford to rent a space.'

I pass the notes to Holly and her eyes skim over my messy handwriting.

She grins. 'I love it!'

TONY

I knock on the open door to the manager's office.

Tony looks up from his desk. 'Hello?'

'Hi, Tony. Could I use your printer? The one on the shop floor has finally snuffed it.'

He blinks. 'Well, is it work related?'

Eugh. Just because he caught me making multiple copies of Phil Mitchell to stick to the inside of Holly's locker *that one time*, he questions this. Guess I'll never live that one down.

'One hundred per cent genuinely work related,' I assure him.

I want to print more copies of our open letter.

It's been shared widely on social media since we posted it, and I'm now thinking of distributing paper copies around the town centre.

'Right, okay then.' Tony gets up out of his chair and hovers while I click around on his desktop.

He's got one of those cork pinboards above his desk. As the printer groans into action, I notice a curled-up photo (I'm guessing it's from the early nineties by the size of his glasses) and in it Tony is holding some sort of award and *actually smiling*. In the short time that I've known him Tony's seemed distracted and stressed and unhappy. An image of him smiling seems so unnatural. Like when you see a baby bird before its feathers have grown. All pink and veiny and bald. Like, you know it's a bird (or your manager) but something just looks *wrong*.

'When was that picture taken, Tony?'

'*What?*' I've irritated him. 'Oh God, years ago. Some awards thing.' He dismisses it by waving his hand, fiddling about with a stack of books that have piled up on top of the filing cabinet.

'What award did you win?'

He mutters something that I can't hear. 'Sorry, what?'

'BOOKSELLER OF THE YEAR.' When he makes eye contact he looks annoyed, then embarrassed.

'Wow. Congratulations!'

'Um, thank you.' He adjusts the broken glasses on the bridge of his nose. That was another little glimpse into the

Secret Tony he keeps under wraps: the former Bookseller of the Year who started out like we all did, as someone with a devotion to those funny things with words and pages in them. Now he's crushed, squashed by management and buckling under the pressure.

Maxine knocks impatiently on the office door and doesn't wait for a response before rushing in. 'Tony, we need you downstairs. One of the elderly gents has had an accident in the armchair. I'm sorry I can't clean it up. Not today. It's a number two.'

Tony holds his silvery head in his hands. 'JESUS CHRIST!'

I'm concerned that he might just explode right there. Then we'd have customer bowels *and* Tony's scrambled innards to clean up. And *neither* of us are prepared to do *that*.

He takes a deep breath and starts tearing through the cupboards to find some cleaning equipment, breathlessly seething. 'This is the *exact* sort of behaviour that head office expects from this branch! People using us as a bloody toilet!'

Maxine and I watch, lips pursed, before Tony eventually comes up with a yellow J-cloth and a bottle of Dettol. Oh dear.

'Right! Show me where it is then!' The two of them bustle out of the office, and leave me here, leaning back in the wheelie chair behind the desk, cool glass of water in hand, as if I'm running the place.

EWWWWWWWWWWWWWWWWWW!!!

Oh God!

Without thinking I sipped from the glass of water only to realise, far too late, that it wasn't my water at all. It wasn't my glass. It was a cup full of Tony's cold, mouldy coffee.

How disgusting! I spit it back into the mug without even thinking about it. I'm gagging and dribbling over the computer keyboard.

Oh *no*, I've swapped *saliva* with Tony. My lips have been where his lips have been.

I look around at the room and recoil in horror at a million dirty mugs, all containing various levels of cold coffee. Dear Lord.

I take a desperate swig of my own uncontaminated drink. An attempt to wash away any Bookshop Manager Bacteria.

The office phone rings.

Oh God. It'll be like those old eighties horror films where hormonal boys morph into werewolves and terrorise the hallways of their high schools. Instead of growing fur all over my hands, my hair will shrink and turn grey. My shoulders will hunch. I'll become bitter and direct all of my grump at teenage bookseller girls.

The phone bleats again. Maybe when I go to answer it, Tony's voice will come out of my mouth? My gross, infected mouth that tastes like three-week-old coffee.

I pick up.

'Hello?' *Phew, I'm still me!* I touch my body, and pat myself down to reassure myself that the poison hasn't finished me off just yet.

'Hello, am I through to Bennett's Bookshop?' A woman's nasaly voice is on the other end of the line.

'Yes, yes, you are. This is Tony Humphreys' office. He's not at his desk right now but I can take a message and ask him to get back to you?' I'd make a brilliant receptionist. I'd wear cute little coords in pastel colours and file my nails between taking calls.

'Right, I'm calling on behalf of the Greysworth Town Council's Petitions Committee . . .'

I slap my free hand over my mouth so stop myself from OMGing out loud and let the lady continue. 'Now, the contact name we have here is *Paige Turner*, but we're not quite sure if that's a pseudonym or an actual member of staff?'

LOL!

'It's me! I'm a real-life member of staff! I'm Paige Turner; it is, unfortunately, my real name.' I laugh, shaking with anticipation.

'Okay, sorry about that, Paige. My name is Judy, I'm just calling to let you know that we've received your petition to protect Bennett's Bookshop from closure and subsequent demolition . . .'

(Pronounced 'demolitiooooooooooon', prolonged in the *most* monotonous drawl.)

'. . . and in response to the volume of signatures you've received we think it's best to organise a consultation to discuss the future of the premises.'

'Okay, wow! Fantastic!' I scramble around on Tony's desk for a biro that actually works. Poised to write down all of the important info.

'So, a meeting will take place next Monday at four o'clock, at Bennett's.'

Without looking at the National Geographic calendar on Tony's wall, I know that next Monday is scheduled to be the day we close for good.

I scribble as Judy talks. 'We need your store manager to attend the meeting, where he will be joined by Mick Morgan, regional manager for Bennett's Bookshops, along with Jeffrey Khan, the landlord of the current premises, and Greg Simmonds, a local politician who has been closely involved with the high-street regeneration scheme.'

Okay . . . I make a list of these new names.

'Now, as you are the person who submitted the petition in the first place, you and your supporters will have a chance to voice your issues and concerns, although I have to inform you that it will be the group of people in that meeting who have the authority to work together to reach a decision.'

'Okay, well, thank you so much for getting back to me, Judy. I appreciate it . . . Bye.'

I put the phone down and sit back in Tony's chair.

This is huge.

This means that in a few days' time, the people who want this place to close will all be here together under one roof. Under *our* roof.

This means that we have a real chance to make a difference. To take action. Direct action.

My mind races and my eyes glaze over at something on Tony's wall.

I blink and notice that it's a signed poster for that Hilary Mackintosh novel he raved on about in Holly's campaign video.

My fingers slam on the keyboard as I frantically log on to the Bennett's Greysworth Twitter page.

I've got it.

OCCUPY BENNETT'S

We sit round the staffroom coffee table. It's covered in tea stains. Like some psychotic snail has been snotting around in circles and leaving a shiny film of grot over the pine.

We've just locked up for the night; it's home time. Usually this is when everybody's busy fetching their bags and rolling cigarettes and Nikki changes out of her comfy shop-floor shoes.

I asked the others if they'd stay behind. Only for a little bit. Just while I tell them about something.

'Okay then . . .' Tony clears his throat and polishes his fragile glasses on the edge of his shirt. 'Paige has some kind of announcement to make . . .'

My fellow booksellers look concerned.

Holly looks like she's accidentally missed an episode

of her fave reality show and is struggling to follow who's slept with who.

'So, earlier today, I took a call while I was in Tony's office . . .'

Adam has folded his copy of the *Guardian* shut and is listening carefully while I tell them all about the meeting that'll be happening right here in a matter of days.

'Oh, and so I'm just finding out about this now? *Great* . . .' Tony mutters.

'What I'm saying is we need to try something while we have these people here, something big . . . a stunt.'

'A *stunt*?!'

'Okay, okay, hear me out. I really think this could work.'

Holly leans forward in her chair, her elbows resting on her knees and she smiles. It's the same smile she flashed at me when we were at primary school and it was my turn to jump in the swimming pool. It's the same smile as when she poured me a shot of sambuca in her kitchen when her mum and dad were out and I hesitated before burning my stomach with it. It's the smile she gives me when she's saying '*Yes, come on, you're fine.*'

'I think that on Monday, the day of the meeting and the last day of trading, we should stay in the shop.'

Blinking. So much blinking. And silence.

'We stage a protest and we *occupy Bennett's*. We'll show them that we don't intend on budging. And we won't leave, not until they have heard us out and reconsider the plan to demolish this place.'

'A *protest*? I don't think so.' Tony flaps around, tidying the sticky, dated issues of the *Bookseller*, which have been sitting here splattered by microwave lunches long before I interviewed for this job. His sudden, unprompted attempt to clear them away is his way of wrapping me up. Of shutting me up. Of dismissing my plan altogether.

My colleagues shuffle uncomfortably in their seats. I try to win the room over. 'It will be a *peaceful* protest, I promise.'

Of course I've thought about the alternatives. I've fantasised about marching those suits up into the staffroom. Holding the ancient price-sticker gun to their heads. Tying them to wheelie chairs with parcel tape. Gagging them with promotional tote bags while we tell them our objectives. I've considered the torture we could inflict by pressing all the buttons on the noisy books from the kids' section until they go insane and cave in.

Of course I've *thought* about it but – 'We need this to work. This is our chance to actually save Bennett's. So we gather supporters, and we sit in, we come together, in a *peaceful, civilised* manner, and make sure that we are taken seriously by the powers that be . . .'

'Oh, come on, Paige,' Tony grumbles. 'Absolutely not.' He picks up the stack of old magazines and dumps them in the recycling bin.

It feels like everything inside me is bubbling. Like that YouTube video Elliot showed me of American kids performing a high-school prank. They shove mints into bottles of cola and stand back as the whole thing erupts. They watch it fizz and whoosh like a sticky, sugary rocket.

'Sorry, Tony . . .' I deliberately want my voice to come out as calm and as even as it possibly can. 'I'm not asking for your permission. It's too late . . .'

I'm standing up to Tony and it's a bit scary. Not because he's particularly 'scary', but he's a grown-up. My boss. It feels risky. I can feel every nerve inside my body twitch.

The fear of everybody here laughing at me, thinking I'm just a silly girl, can't stall me now.

I tell Holly I need to borrow her phone, and with no questions asked she hands it over. I'm tapping at it with my thumbs while my manager sighs impatiently.

'Look, Tony!'

He squints at the screen. It's a tweet from Hilary Mackintosh to Bennett's Greysworth.

'But she's-she's my favourite writer . . .' he whispers in disbelief.

'And she's coming here. To Bennett's. To the protest on Monday.' I hope this changes Tony's mind.

'Doesn't she live miles away . . . in the Shetlands or something?'

'Yeah, she does. But after I messaged her this afternoon and told her all about the campaign, she's agreed to travel all that way to come here. She's doing it to support us, Tony. So say you will too? Please?'

His face physically changes; it melts from something hard into something soft.

'We need you on our side.'

'Hilary Mackintosh? Coming *here*?!' His eyes dart around the dingy staffroom, as though he's seeing the place for the first time. 'Okay.'

I clench my fists. *Yes!*

Tony nods and scratches his grey head in consideration. 'Just *as long as* you *promise* to keep everything under control . . .' he warns.

'Get in!' Adam's on his feet punching the hot air.

'You're a devious genius!' Holly squeals into my ear, as she flings her arms round my shoulders.

'Let's occupy Bennett's!'

We're doing this.

THE JAMES DEAN OF
OFFICE AND STATIONERY SUPPLIES

It's Sunday. I pat my fringe into place as I check my reflection in the glass door to Coleman's Stationers. I push my way in and hope that Blaine is working today.

There's no immediate sign of him. I tunnel my way through the ring binders and fountain pens, the left-handed scissors and pots of Tipp-Ex, to the photocopier at the back of the shop.

There he is, sitting behind the counter, wearing *that* uniform, sharpening some pencils.

I clear my throat and he looks up. 'Hi.'

'Oh, hey, Paige. How's it going?'

'Good, thanks.' I smile. 'I just need some stuff photocopied actually . . .' I start getting my paper in order when he gets up out of his seat and leans forward over the counter.

'Okay.' His voice is low. He's whispering to me. 'So, I'm actually banned from using the copier, but seeing as it's you and it's for a good cause . . . I'm willing to risk an official warning for it.' That dimple. A puncture in his otherwise perfect face. I want to dive into that dimple head first and live inside it.

'Thanks, I appreciate it!' It's all I can cough out at this point. He's banned! He's a rule-breaker! A tearaway! A Rebel without a cause! The James Dean of Office and Stationery Supplies. He's an *anarchist*.

'So why are you banned from using the photocopier?' I ask. So bold. Internal pat on the back as I try my hardest to suppress the pure excitement that has taken hold of my whole body.

'Oh, I was using it for my own personal projects.' He pauses and nods his head. 'Nudes.'

Oh dear Lord. I'm stunned into silence. Nudes. Nudity. I just stare. I try really hard not to stare at his body. His body that has the option to be nude.

I wonder if they were pictures of Naked Sue. Or Correctum.

The mental image of Correctum's naked cracked heels momentarily cools me down, until Blaine starts pressing the buttons on the machine and it hums and it comes to life. 'It was all for artistic purposes, though, I promise. My boss found them and now she thinks I'm some kind of sick deviant.'

His smile is too wide for his face. It's blinding.

I pass the master copies of the flyers and posters across the desk and watch his eyes flash over my hand-drawn type. SAVE BENNETT'S DEMO AND OCCUPATION. SUPPORT YOUR LOCAL BOOKSHOP.

'What's going on then?'

He looks serious and studies me as I blabber on and on about the sit-in.

'You should come along.' I try to make it sound casual. Like I'm not bothered either way. Like it's not the biggest thing I've planned since my thirteenth birthday party at the ice rink.

'Okay, sure. I'll be there.'

Get in! I'll be occupying Bennett's with Beautiful Blaine Henderson by my side. Perfection.

'Hey, come round here.' He invites me behind the desk, closer to the copier, and to him, and I do not need to be asked twice. 'So what do you need? Double-sided? One-sided?'

'The posters are one-sided A3 . . . and for the zines I need double A4 . . .'

'Oh, you're making zines? Nice.'

'Thanks.' The beams of light pass under the lid and as he hunches his shoulders his hair falls into his eyes.

This is too good to be true. It's just me and him, held together in this world of fluoro highlighters and poster paints.

His eyes meet mine and I'm pretty sure I visibly melt in front of him.

To distract myself I pick up a nearby packet of glittery dolphin stickers and shimmy them in the light.

'These are so cool. I love dolphins.' I giggle, impressed at what the Coleman's sticker game has to offer.

'Yeah? Doesn't everyone love dolphins?'

I roll my eyes. 'C'mon! That's it exactly: everybody loves them, they think they're so friendly and cute, but a quick Google search can prove what slippery bastards they really are! You know they turn nasty and eat humans, right?'

'Have them. Go on, take them. On the house.'

'Really?' I hold the shiny dolphins to my heart.

'You can't have a zine without stickers anyway; it just wouldn't be right.'

The copies are ready; they shoot out of the machine, hot off the press.

I pass him a ten-pound note and he hands me the change.

I try to avoid fixating on the brief hand-to-hand contact. 'So I'll see you tomorrow, comrade?'

'Yeah.' A mischievous grin spreads across his face as he says, 'I've got an idea.'

'Really?! What?'

'Just leave it with me.'

SWIMMING WITH DOLPHINS

'*Every little girl dreams of being a princess on her wedding day . . .*'

'Do *not!*' I shout at the telly as the intro to another episode of *Nightmare Brides* zooms past. Mum fast-forwards; we've seen this programme so many times that we skip to the dress tantrum. Predictable as it always is. A woman with a lisp squeezes herself into a vile strapless monstrosity.

'*Will it be a fairy-tale ending?*'

'Doubt it.' Mum throws a scrunched-up biscuit wrapper towards the screen and we both laugh.

'Are you watching this *again?*' Elliot steps into the room carefully carrying a hot mug of tea for Mum. He's got both hands cupped round its sides and stares into the not-too-milky-please brew like it's telling his fortune.

The bride is sobbing over her pratty fiancé's choice of

dress and the three of us tut.

'Jesus!' The hand-me-down Nokia that Mum donated to me since my beloved iPhone was nicked vibrates and polyphonically bleats full volume.

'I know. Get a grip, love; if you're this disappointed by him based on his choice of dress, why bother marrying him?' Mum shakes her head as she sips her tea.

It's Alison Weaver from the *Chronicle*, the human equivalent of a Rich Tea biscuit, confirming that she'll be at the occupation tomorrow.

I reply with an old-school smiley face.

Great! :-)

Elliot smirks at me. 'By the way, Paige, Otzi called.'

'What?' I scowl, because I think he's taking the mick. 'Who's Otzi?'

'Y'know, Otzi the Iceman. He died in the Stone Age. His body was frozen and naturally mummified for thousands of years.'

I roll my eyes at Mum. 'Right, so what do you mean he called?'

'He wants you to give him his phone back!' he howls, pointing to the artefact I type out a reply to Alison on.

All I can come back with is: 'Ha ha, very funny.'

Elliot: one. Paige: nil.

The three of us turn back to the telly, where the father of the bride is crying. '*I've never felt so proud.*'

Of what? Your daughter *marrying* someone? Oh, pur-lease. Like a marriage contract to say that she 'belongs' to another man is her greatest achievement. This woman is a *veterinary surgeon* for God's sake! She's performed surgery on a cow. They have four stomachs! Her marriage to some loser with a neck tattoo should not be her defining moment.

I narrow my eyes and think hard about what I'd like my defining moment to be.

Maybe it will be tomorrow night. The occupation.

Yeah, I quite like that idea . . . *Paige Turner, High-street Heroine . . . Saviour of the Written Word . . .*

'I'm gonna run upstairs and pack my bag for tomorrow,' I explain to my family, before my brother pipes up.

'But you haven't even seen the reception venue yet!'

He likes this programme way more than he lets on.

Cross-legged on my bedroom floor I gather provisions for my Occupation Survival Kit.

Face wipes: check.

Eyeliner, hairspray, *Party Girl Pink* lipstick: check.

Spare pair of knickers, box of cereal bars: check.

SAVE BENNETT'S T-shirt: check.

Pillow and sleeping bag . . . ?

I delve under my bed for my sleeping bag and pull at the unopened padded envelope I shoved under here the other week. The day that we found out Bennett's was closing.

I tear at the brown paper and pull out a shiny new prospectus.

I trace my fingers over the gold embossing. *Cambridge School of Art.*

I slowly flick through the pages, past examples of students' work, photographs of bright, airy painting studios, of stone turrets and arty lecturers with waxed moustaches. Imagine being allowed to do nothing but draw for three years. Dream. Come. True. I want to dive into that world. I want to live in the insides of this pamphlet.

I just need to get there. I just need a place on a course. I just need the money. I just need a job.

I just need everything to work out tomorrow.

Oh God, I really hope people turn up to the protest.

It would be pretty embarrassing if nobody bothered to come along.

What if it's a complete failure and nobody shows?

That would be the *worst*.

I'd be trapped here forever. In this town. No bright, airy studios. No stone turrets or gold embossing.

I feel the blood drain from my face and start to panic.

I climb into bed.

I lie very still on my back and stare up at the ceiling. It's a funny texture. Like the meringues they make on *Bake Off*. I think it's called Artex.

I look up at the chalky shadows and spikes and swirls and try to slow down my breathing.

'Please, please, let tomorrow work out,' I whisper. I have no idea who I'm talking to.

I roll onto my side and spot the sheet of glittery dolphin stickers Blaine gave me earlier today.

They're lying on the floor. Smiling and winking, static and silent. I stretch to pick them up and wiggle the sheet above my face, watching their shiny fins shimmer.

Blaine Henderson. What a babe.

Holly isn't a fan.

But, oh God, I am.

Is it *really* such a huge deal if your best friend thinks the boy you worship is a bit of a dick?

What do the dolphins have to say about it? *'Blaine is cute! Holly's wrong about him!'*

He looked so fit when I saw him today.

That dimple he gets when he smirks.

Those hands. Magic hands. Drawing Naked Sue. Flicking through the pages of his sketchbook. Passing me cute stickers.

I relive our conversation at the photocopier.

How close he was standing next to me.

I hope he turns up tomorrow.

Maybe it wouldn't actually be so bad if no one else bothered, as long as he did.

Then it could be just me and him.

Me and him locked in the bookshop.

Overnight.

That's a delicious thought.

Imaginary conversations take over.

How I'd laugh and he'd laugh and how his hands felt on my skin that day we danced to Bobby the Busker.

Those glittery dolphins swim me to a very, very happy place.

I lie in bed and live out the fantasy of being locked in the shop with him.

Again and again.

And again.

I'm completely submerged in it. All knickers and hands

and humidity. When my phone beeps.

My clammy fingers tap at the keypad to see who the message is from.

Holly.

Don't forget your toothbrush! Xxxxx

I get up on my feet, sweaty. Smooth my hair and exhale. Drop my toothbrush into my Occupation Survival Kit. 'Check.'

OCCUPATION DAY

It's a good turnout. Familiar faces fill the shop. There are plenty of people from school. Even a few of my teachers who look plain *weird*, standing around in their jeans and trainers, trying to convince us all that they are real-life human beings outside the classroom. The Posers life-drawing crowd have gathered. Well, all of them except Blaine. I guess he must be on his way. I recognise the shop assistants from Lush and the checkout boys from Tesco Express in the crowd. Even some of the lads from the phone shop have rolled up in a haze of overpowering aftershave.

There are customers who are genuinely upset at the thought of losing this place and are willing to stay here overnight to make a point. They chatter to one another, leafing through hardbacks and leaning on placards.

It proves all of my doubts wrong. Any concerns I had about this being a flop seem pretty ridiculous now, when we have a whole *collective* of bookshop lovers supporting the cause.

Tony gushes as his literary heroine, Hilary Mackintosh, secures the lid back onto a Sharpie. She's just signed his entire collection of her novels. Spines creased. Pages thumbed. Old faves.

Alison, the journalist from the *Chronicle*, is back at Bennett's to cover today's action. She's screwing a huge shiny lens onto her fancy camera.

I watch the door anxiously. Waiting for them to arrive.

Amidst the crowd of bookshop protestors, of placards painted with literary puns, of home-made vegan snacks and happy people sipping wine from plastic cups, I see the three men who plan to shut us down arrive. They move in single file towards Tony and take it in turns to shake his hand.

Mick Morgan looks unnecessarily intimidated by the mass of bookish types as he welcomes Jeffrey Kahn and Greg Simmonds to Bennett's Greysworth, one of the shops he is responsible for as regional manager.

My stomach flips as Holly appears next to me, laughing nervously. 'What do we, like, *do* now that all these people are here?'

'Paige! Take this!' Adam passes me an *actual* megaphone, his skinny arms exposed by his SAVE BENNETT'S T-shirt.

'What's all this?' I hear Mick ask Tony, as he watches me climb onto the nearest kick stool. He clasps his hands together in front of him, like a footballer protecting his 'manhood' from a free kick.

'Hello.' This thing makes my voice feel massive. 'Can I have your attention, please?' I wasn't even planning on saying that; I feel like the megaphone made me do it. I look out at the crowd and feel myself wobble. Holly is right by my side, wrapping her arm behind my knees, supporting me and giving me a gentle *you can do it* squeeze.

I suddenly notice the toddlers who are sitting on their parents' shoulders, their small round heads popping up above the crowd of grown-ups. Down by my feet, there's an adorable little girl. She's probably about eight and she has bright orange hair. She's got a placard stuck to the handlebars of her scooter. She frowns at me as she clutches a Pippi Longstocking book in her little hands.

What would Pippi do, right?

Okay, here we go.

I unfold the scrap of paper I scribbled my notes onto late last night, and my hands shake as I read it.

It's just everybody you've ever known, Paige. You're

only making the most important speech of your life so far. Chill, dude. *No biggie.*

'Hello, everybody!' My voice wavers with nerves. I cough to clear my throat, and it echoes through the megaphone, deafening everybody in the front row. 'Thank you to everyone who has come here today to show your solidarity and support . . . It means so much to me and my friends to see such a huge, happy turnout . . .' *Yes, Paige, you can do this.* 'I'd like to welcome Mick Morgan, Jeffrey Khan and Greg Simmonds to our demonstration. Today is about saving Bennett's. Tomorrow will be about saving Bennett's. And if needs be, the day *after* tomorrow will also be about saving Bennett's. This is an occupation, a sit-in protest. We will sit down to stand up for our bookshop. Our objective is clear: we reject the plans, laid out by the high-street regeneration scheme, to close us down so that this building can be demolished.'

The crowd start to hiss and boo. It's all very panto. Maybe Tony will resurface after the meeting, dressed as a dame or the arse-end of a horse.

'We would appreciate it if today an alternative plan could be put forward. An alternative that saves this bookshop. The only bookshop in this town. The bookshop that attracted one thousand people to sign the petition to keep us here.' There's a cheer from my colleagues. 'An alternative to the plans for "regeneration", which are, so far, pushing our only access to new books out of this town.' I nod towards Tony and the men in suits and clench my fist, punching the dusty air. 'SAVE BENNETT'S BOOKSHOP!'

Sue starts chanting '*What do we want? BOOKS! When do we want them? FOREVER!*' and it catches on with a pocket of people around her.

I climb down from my soapbox, flustered. I think my nerves got the better of me. I don't know if I'll ever feel that I've said enough to make a difference. I'm too busy suffocating in a crush of hugs to dwell on that right now, though.

Tony leads the suits upstairs to his office, and as they pass by Maxine offers a paper plate of veggie samosas their way. Mick flinches. 'Oh! No! No, thank you.'

Now all we can do is wait, I suppose.

SITTING IN

Things have taken a surreal turn.

Sue's arms are above her head. Her pinky-brown nipples look like a sad pug's eyes staring in opposite directions.

Elspeth crouches and flips her sketchbook open.

'Spontaneous Posers class!' Jamie fist-pumps the hot air.

'Oh no.' Elspeth waves a silver-ringed finger. 'This isn't life drawing, this is *Reportage*.'

Reportage because this is *really* happening. Sue is taking direct action, as promised. I didn't expect direct action to be quite so . . . *nipple-y*, but when I saw Sue standing on top of a display plinth, unbuttoning her blouse and hollering 'TRY TO IGNORE *THIS*, HIGH-STREET REGENERATORS! BENNETT'S IS HERE TO STAY!' I was so moved by her solidarity, and her armpit stubble, that I joined in with the crowd's applause.

'Um, is she *allowed* to do that in here?!' Adam hisses through gritted teeth, his cheeks flushing as he does everything in his power to avoid looking directly at Sue's curves.

Sue '*ahem*'s to grab the teensy-weensy bit of attention that was off her for a split second. 'I may not be "*allowed*" to do this; "*society*" might tell me to keep my knickers on, but this is an act of civil disobedience.'

I'm pretty sure she's breaking some kind of unspoken rule about nudity on the shop floor, but, hey, it's classic Sue. A group of protesters have already gathered around her feet and are picking up pencils and paper to get involved with the sketching sesh.

I guess I shouldn't have expected any less from inviting the Posers crowd. Clive must recognise that feeling on my face as he leans over and chuckles. 'Life models, eh? Can't take them anywhere!'

He's obvs not fazed by the full-frontal nudity sitch; he makes his way over to the table and begins to pour himself a plastic cup of bargain wine. 'They're taking their time up there, aren't they? How long's it been now?'

'About an hour . . .' I reply, all too aware we still haven't had an answer from Mick Morgan and the gang. I do my best to ignore the knots twisting in my stomach.

'Oh! Look who it is!' Clive's crusty artist hand (aka one of his 'tools') waves to someone just behind me.

Sweet Baby Beyoncé on a bike! It's Blaine. It's my photocopying, life-drawing, sticker-donating bae.

He's later than he promised, and he's dressed head to toe in black with a group of four other boys.

JUST A BIT OF PUBLIC DISORDER

'What have they come dressed as?' Holly raises her eyebrows and just as I'm about to rush over to Blaine to say hi, something stops me. One of the boys he's with has a balaclava pulled over his face.

Why would anyone wear a balaclava unless they were about to rob a ban—

SMASH.

Blaine hurls a brick through the Bennett's display window.

There's glass everywhere. The crowd of peaceful protesters stagger backwards away from the boys who tear through the window, trashing the place.

What the hell?!

'Stop! Stop it!' I yell, grabbing the lad with the balaclava as he pushes a table of non-fiction over. Paperbacks slide over the shop floor that has descended into chaos.

Blaine scoops armfuls of books into a holdall, not even looking at what he's taking.

'What's going on?! What do you think you're doing?!' I shout at him over the racket from the shop full of people screaming, panicking, dialling 999.

He holds his hands in the air triumphantly. 'This is a riot! This is anarchy!'

'Don't be so *ridiculous*!' I screech. Fuming. How could he do this? How could he do this *to me*?! There is so much at stake and he's blowing it.

He laughs. 'Paige, chill. It's just a bit of public disorder. Looting. That's all. You want publicity, don't you?'

'No!' I despair. *Looting*? Who would *loot* an effing bookshop?!

His mate, some tall guy with an ironic handlebar moustache and a black roll-neck, shrugs and asks, 'Who is she anyway?' as he side-eyes me, like *I'm* the one who's in the wrong place at the wrong time. 'I mean, it's not like it's the first time you've nicked stuff from here.'

'What?! Blaine?!' What does this guy mean? Does he really mean that *Blaine* has been stealing from Bennett's all along? I think of Tony studying the stock loss figures. I think of Mr Barnes stuffing books down his trousers. In a flash I start to question everything I think I know about this boy.

'This isn't the *first* time you've nicked stuff from here?' I ask again to clarify. Just for *some* clarity. Just a tiny, *miniscule* scrap of certainty in this completely mental situation.

Blaine rolls his eyes, exasperated by my perfectly reasonable question. 'I'm not *stealing*, am I? I'm just reclaiming my right to have access to literature from *The Man*. C'mon, Paige, join the revolution.' His mouth curls into a smile, like he has actually fooled himself into thinking he knows what he's talking about.

'That's bullshit!' I thunder. '*The Man?! I'm* not The Man. *I'm* not even *A MAN*! I'm supposed to be your friend!'

I immediately cringe when I hear myself say 'fwend' like a baby and his friends laugh at me.

'Seriously, though, who is she?' The bloke who looks like he belongs on a packet of Pringles asks this *again*, while he takes a selfie. Yep, that's right, a *selfie*, as he commits an actual crime. This is the calibre of self-centred imbeciles I'm dealing with right now.

'I don't know *what* you think you're achieving, Blaine, but you won't get away with this. The police will be on their way.'

He snorts. Laughs at me. *Laughs right in my face.*

Of course. I think about what he said about that day at the fountain. *Eugh, that bloody day at the fountain!* That he isn't threatened by the police. The 'pigs' or 'puppets' or whatever he refers to them as when he's trying to sound like a tough guy. Like the James Dean of Office and Art Supplies.

Blaine Henderson isn't scared of the police. He's not scared of hurting my feelings.

Luckily I know exactly what he *is* scared of.

I clench my fist and pound the fire alarm I'm standing next to. Breaking the glass makes my knuckles bleed and it also sets the sprinkler system into action.

Cold water sprays from the ceiling and the sirens wail.

The crowd of protesters who hadn't bustled past this mob of idiotic vandals before, run for the door, out onto the dry pavement.

I turn to the boy with the moustache and the bad selfie habit. 'Oh, and before you ask again, I'll tell you *who I am.*' I point at my chest, at my home-made SAVE BENNETT'S T-shirt. 'My *name* is Paige.'

Tony and the suits scramble down the stairs from their meeting and are met by carnage.

'What the *hell* is going on?!'

Blaine cowers from the shower and tries to protect his

precious hair with his hands.

I can't believe this is the same boy I've been lusting after for weeks. He doesn't look gorgeous now. He doesn't look cool. He looks like a frigging idiot.

'What are you *doing*?!' he asks me, picking up an actual book to shelter his head with.

'What am *I* doing?! *Me*? Oh, *nothing much*, just trying to save the place you're obviously hell bent on *destroying*! What's the matter with you?!' I snatch the book from him and wait for an answer. He doesn't say anything immediately so I can't help but continue. 'What were you *thinking* of smashing the window for? It's right next to the door and *the door was open*!' He's edging away from me, pacing backwards through the broken glass and out onto the street. 'Blaine, how could you do this? You don't even care about the demonstration or the campaign, do you? How *could* you care, when you've been helping yourself to free books all along? You made this about you, but today is about so much more than you. This is about real people, and our jobs.'

We stand on the other side of the broken window, on the high street.

'So much was resting on today going well, and we've worked so hard together to make it happen . . .' I blink away the prickly feeling behind my eyes.

'I *need* this job, Blaine. I need the money to get out of this dump. This dump, which is about to become a whole lot *dumpier* if we lose the only good thing about it. Do you have any idea what it will mean for this high street if we close? It's hugely unlikely that anyone will bother opening up a different bookshop once one has failed. It will make this place a *complete* cultural wasteland.

'Books are more than just a prop to pose around with when you're trying to convince people you've got a bit of substance. Books are an escape route. A refuge. They can be a connection to a stranger, someone you've never met, who writes something that you hadn't considered anyone in the world to have felt but you. When you grow up feeling too big for a place, and you make that kind of connection with a book, it's like a link; it's a tunnel to the outside world. A glimmer of something *beyond*. If we lose Bennett's, then we block all of those tunnels. We slam all of those doors.

'There's a whole universe outside your little bubble of Blaine, and your pathetic attempt at "anarchy" might have just cost us everything we've been campaigning for.

'I thought you were cool, but you're not. You're nothing but a poser. Please, just get lost. And if, by some freak chance, Bennett's is saved, don't bother coming back.'

I stop to breathe and follow his eyes. Dark blue eyes that, up until now, made me look at him the way I look at the chocolate counter in Costcutter when I'm on my period. Those eyes dart around the audience of people watching us.

They're all here, standing and blinking.

Everyone.

I was so lost in ranting at Blaine that I had no idea anybody was listening to me lay into him.

Holly's hands cover her mouth in shock. Jamie holds his phone up, recording the whole thing as Adam switches off the sprinkler system.

A camera flashes loudly, as Alison, the reporter from the local paper, paps Blaine.

'No! No photos!' he protests, attempting to hide his ruined, dripping-wet hair from the lens. I watch as he legs it up the high street and into the distance.

Tony strategically places a rather soggy cardboard Mary Berry in front of Sue's naked body. Mr Abbott is wrapped in one of those emergency tinfoil blankets, like a jacket potato from the school canteen.

People walking along the pavement, laden with Primark shopping bags, buggies and Happy Meals stop to see what all the commotion is about.

'This is exactly what we've just been discussing. That this is *not* the sort of town that wants a bookshop. You'd prefer to . . . to *riot* than read . . .' Mick Morgan gesticulates furiously with his big hands and Tony shakes his head in disagreement and shame.

'Now hang on there, Mick,' Greg Simmonds, the politician in the navy blazer, pipes up. 'I think that what this young lady has just shown us is how much a town like this can benefit from a bookshop. Readers make a better society. That's the kind of thing I want for Greysworth town.'

I shiver in my damp SAVE BENNETT'S T-shirt, folding my arms across my chest, waiting for him to continue.

'Realistically I don't think that at this point, there's any chance of us getting away from the fact that the demolition will go ahead. It's scheduled for the near future and I do believe that modern retail units will benefit our town centre in the long run.' Greg explains this to us and my heart breaks. '*But*, Paige, is it? What you've just said has clarified a lot of things for me. I think it's crucial that the people of Greysworth have access to a bookshop. Thanks to you, I will continue discussions with Mick and Jeffrey, and we will do our utmost to secure a future for Bennett's on this high street.'

OMG!

Mr Kahn, the landlord shrugs and strokes the back of his neck. 'I suppose we could look into the numbers again . . . We could try to reach a compromise with the rent, keeping it affordable. Give Bennett's a chance . . .' he offers.

Is he saying what I think he's saying?

Did we – Did this *work*?

'We haven't reached an official solution yet but . . .' Simmonds smiles. 'But I'd like to congratulate you on all of your hard work during this campaign.'

'Well, let's shake on it!' I demand, before squeezing on the clammy hands of all the men in suits, my knuckles still bleeding and sore from the fire alarm.

Tony cups his hands around his face in disbelief. 'I can't believe it! It actually worked. All of this –' he looks towards the shattered glass and the wet carpet and the home-made placards – 'the petition, the protest, it seems to have done the trick.' He smiles. Happy tears well up behind his broken glasses.

'Paige!' Holly grabs me. 'You were fierce! Yes, girl! We did it!' She plants a triumphant Barry M kiss on my cheek.

I still can't quite believe it. She's right!

We've done it.

Immediately after smooching me, Holly turns to Jamie and kisses him too; she pulls him towards her and they snog for about twenty minutes. *OMG, get in there, Hols.*

Somebody blasts Kool & The Gang 'Celebrate' through tinny phone speakers and the gaggle of soggy protestors erupt into cheers.

I stand with my back against the broken shop window and watch them party. In the film adaptation of my life, this is the sentimental end scene, isn't it? Everything would be shot in soft focus and move in slow motion. I'd be right here, misty-eyed, watching a shop full of quiet, bookish types, who turned out to be pretty hardcore demonstrators, dance and sing and laugh and cry.

A voiceover would echo as the disco classic fades out. I'd make some kind of observation about how '*As lame as I expected it to be, sticking around in this bumhole of a town all summer has taught me a few things. One: sulky arty boys who hang around in bookshops aren't necessarily all they're cracked up to be. Two: drawing boobs and bums and hands and feet isn't much different from drawing wax fruit with Mr Parker, but Sue and the rest of the Posers crowd turned out to be way more fascinating than that dusty bunch of grapes. And three: turns out that people are ready to listen to what a bookshop girl with a bad fringe has to say after all. I just had to believe in myself until they did too . . .*

GAG.

As the credits roll and Sue waddles towards me, offering me a soggy paper plate of Quorn sausage rolls, a lad on a bike pedals by and yells at the top of his smoke-damaged lungs, 'BOOKSHOP TOSSERRRRRRS!'

We all clap and cheer him.

Wheeeeeeey!

He wobbles on his wheels and screws up his face, before speeding along the road, away from our butt-kickin' bookshop-saving gang.

THREE MONTHS LATER

'Make sure no one's coming!' I hiss at Holly, who's standing behind me, keeping a lookout.

I crouch on the floor with a Sharpie poised; I think I've found the perfect spot, just behind the cash desk, like in the old place.

This new shop is beautiful. It's clean and bright and airy. It smells like wood and paint, like the basement in IKEA. It has a fluffy new carpet that actually springs beneath your feet. The bookshelves are sturdy and have these theatre-style spotlights pointing at them.

We are in the process of setting up to open next week. Me and Holly have volunteered to help out before we go to Posers this evening. There are crates and crates of exciting new books waiting to be discovered. Cardboard boxes of things we brought along from the old shop; plus the kettle and the microwave and the tills and the framed, signed posters and the picture from the newspaper of us all standing outside on the high street. In a rare moment of public sentimentality Tony said he'd frame it to hang on display.

The new Bennett's is beautiful, but it wouldn't be the same without a little bit of bookseller graffiti, would it?

My tongue juts out in concentration as I make my mark in honour of the old shop.

I hear Holly rummage through a box, and remind her to be on guard.

'What's this?' she asks, reading the address on a padded envelope. 'FAO Paige Turner, Bennett's Bookshop, Greysworth. God, it weighs a ton!'

It must be another uni prospectus. More fancy embossing, more course descriptions, more plans. I mentally run through the list of destinations it could take me to. London. Brighton. Manchester. Glasgow.

'That's weird, though.' I frown, my knees clicking. 'All the other brochures I've sent for have been delivered to my house . . . not here . . .'

Holly shrugs and tears at the brown paper.

She blinks. She won't stop blinking at what's inside.

Now she's screeching.

And jumping up and down like she needs a wee.

'What is it, Hol?!' I ask, baffled and still crouching on the floor. I haven't seen her this excited since we spotted Blaine Henderson doing community service. As gorge as I once believed him to be, high-vis yellow is not his colour and he cannot make picking up litter behind Argos look hot.

She shakes her head in disbelief and reads from a small piece of card.

'Dear Paige,
Thank you for your email. I'm so sorry to hear about
your bookshop closing. I think it's a great shame
that we are losing so many bookshops and libraries
up and down the country, and I think it's hugely
commendable that you and your friends are trying to
challenge that. As for your friend Holly, it's always
humbling to hear that readers enjoy my books. Please
find enclosed a copy of the finished manuscript for the
final instalment of the I'm a Murderer trilogy. It is for
Holly to read, enjoy and write all over!
Best of luck,
Paula Williamson.'

Wow!

That's amazing! I never thought she'd actually –

'Paige!' Holly has huge tears in her eyes, as she runs her fingers over the handwritten note over and over, to check that it's real and not a hologram or a mirage. Then she cries some more and laughs hysterically. 'I can't believe you did this! I love you, you absolute nutter!'

She clambers up behind me and squeezes me as I hold my Sharpie poised in position . . .

I can feel my knees buckle and try to hold my hand steady as I scrawl . . .

'*ONE DAY I'LL WRITE A BOOK ABOUT THIS PLA—*'

I know I have to be quick, though. Tony would kill me if he –

'Crap! Paige, be careful!'

'What the HELL are you DOING, Paige?!'

Uh-oh.

I turn round to see him standing there, veins bulging out of his head. He delves into one of the cardboard boxes, rummages around inside and produces that same old bottle of Dettol and same old yellow J-cloth that were used to clean up after the OAP armchair incident.

Well, it may be a shiny new shop, but I guess some things will never change.

BOOKSHOP BINGO

I hope that, like Paige, you are lucky enough to have a bookshop near you. Obviously they're my favourite places to lurk and observe. Here's a list of things to spot in your local one. If you get a full house, don't shout 'FULL HOUSE' – you won't be removed but you'll probably be nicknamed by staff. Instead treat yourself to a shiny new read.

An abandoned reading list	A book about Egon Schiele (Paige's fave freaky nudes)	The Women's Studies section (delve in and find something new – you won't be disappointed. Well, you might be disappointed. At social injustice more than anything else though.)
A cardboard cut-out of a celeb author (disclaimer: no matter how friendly they may appear, cardboard cut outs will *not* help you in a cutie-related-crisis.)	A book with a skeleton on the cover	Somebody sitting on the floor reading
A bookseller trying to write their own novel on the sly	A man picking his nose who thinks nobody can see him picking his nose (rumbled!)	A FITTIE. Depending on where you live this can be a very special, very rare occasion.

Read on for a sneak peek at
Paige's next adventures . . .

Book two coming soon!

LET'S GO GIRLS

'Crap! I totally forgot to pack sun cream!' My best friend Holly panics through a mouthful of Cool Original Doritos, sunglasses sliding down her nose.

I squint at the gloomy clouds through the window of the train and wave goodbye to stinky old Greysworth, which is shrinking further and further into the distance away from us.

'Holly. Look around. It's October. I don't think you'll need your factor fifty.'

'It's not a real holiday without the *smell* of sunblock though, is it?'

'Well . . . we could just pretend that we're on some chic city break. And that we've packed trunks filled with vintage fur coats and Dr Zhivago hats . . .' I glaze over, imagining that the rows of patio gardens and abandoned trampolines whizzing by are actually snow-covered pine trees.

I mean, really, it's not like we're not about to catch a plane to some wild bender in Magaluf or set sail on a once-in-a-lifetime, all-expenses-paid, trip around the Caribbean like the ones you can win on telly competitions.

Nope.

It's way cooler than that.

Me and Holly have blagged ourselves half term at the Skegton-on-Sea Book Festival!

It's one of the biggest book festivals in the country; authors and journalists and TV presenters flock from all over to be there. Apparently tickets *always* sell out within the first hour of going on sale because they have such high-profile guests.

I found that out the hard way, staring in disbelief as the SOLD OUT message flashed on my phone screen in the middle of a French lesson.

'*Ça va, Paige?*' Monique, the class *assistante* asked as she knelt beside the bubble-gum encrusted desk, watching me groan in despair. I mean, it was all *her* fault. If she hadn't picked on me to join her in some cringy role-play *a la pharmacie*, then I'd have snagged tickets for me and Holly before it was too late, rather than wasted precious moments of my life making up the French word for 'Strepsils'.

We had been so prepared. The events programme had been announced weeks ahead of tickets going on sale and as soon as we heard that our all-time favourite (and most dreamy) hot-shot author was flying in to do a talk and promote his brand new graphic novel, we knew we had to be there, front and centre.

Tickets for the whole week cost one hundred pounds. That's right, one *hundred* pounds. One hundred and *one pounds fifty* if you count the booking fee. Think of all the millions of Freddo Frogs and penny sweets you could blow that on.

We both work part time at Bennett's Bookshop, and signed up to all the extra hours we could get just so we had enough money for those tickets. We unpacked crates of heavy new books before college. We vacuumed the shop after the last dawdlers had left the building and we even missed Gracie Partridge's rainy birthday BBQ just so that we earned double pay on the bank holiday weekend. But all for nothing . . .

After we lost out on tickets, we were gutted for approximately an hour and a half, until lunch break that same day. But as we slumped on blue wheelie chairs in the common room, I had an idea.

'We *will* get there, Holly.'

'How do you mean?' she gasped as she burnt the roof

of her mouth on a baked-bean panini (one of our school canteen's delicacies).

'Think about it; we are Bookshop Girls! Books are what we *do*! If we can't get into the festival as fans, then we'll get in there as *booksellers*. As industry *insiders*.'

She nodded, eyes wide and cheeks stuffed like a hamster before swallowing a hot lump of cheesy beans dramatically. 'Maybe Tony knows somebody at the festival who could sort us out . . .'

It turned out that our grumpy bookshop boss *did* know the woman who coordinates *SBF* (as those in the know call it). They went '*way back*' according to Tony, who shifted uncomfortably and adjusted his glasses as we begged him to put our names forward. He *ummed* and *ahhed* at first. *It's a lot of hard work. Really full on. It's not like Greysworth.* He said he wasn't sure it was a good idea, seeing as both of us are still under eighteen. There might not be someone on hand to supervise us. He didn't know if we'd cope.

I reminded him that we're very mature for our age *and* beyond capable *and* that I was told by my orthodontist that I only have to wear my retainer three nights a week, which technically makes me a WOMAN, and he squirmed and said he'd see what he could do and the rest is history.

We'll be manning the bookstalls, selling the relevant novels to festival bookworms and setting up stock to be signed by Big Shot Writers. It's basically like we're being PAID to go on a BFF HOL and SELL A FEW BOOKS! GET IN!

We've never actually been on holiday together before. Well, not if you don't count the residential trip to Milton Keynes Outdoor Adventure Centre in Year Six. That was different. We didn't really *want* to spend a week building rafts while teachers wore jeans and hoodies, masquerading as Normal Human Beings. What's so normal about building a *raft* anyway? This will be way better. Our first hol. Just the two of us. Not a sick bucket in sight.

'I wonder what our Festival Boss will be like . . .' Holly opens the true crime paperback she's obsessing over.

'Tony didn't give much away. Let's just hope she loves Spontaneous Karaoke Without the Actual Backing Tracks and celeb spotting as much as we do.'

'Oh, I have something for you to add to The List,' my partner in crime announces, making grabby movements with her fingers for me to pass her my sketchbook.

I pop the clasp on my new-old suitcase.

I bought it in a charity shop especially for this holiday. It's a vintage powder-blue hat box with a rubber handle. I cleaned the outside of it with a face wipe. The inside is made of fabric so there wasn't much I could do there but spritz a bit of perfume around and hope it didn't make my clothes smell like the manky old cuddly toys in Save the Children.

My notebook is squashed inside the case; it's all dog eared. The List is scrawled inside the notebook.

'*Find out if Tony and our festival Boss were romantically involved.*'

Ew. Holly's such a creep sometimes. One of the many reasons we're soulmates.

We drew up a list of things we want to see/eat/Instagram while we're on this hol. The list is constantly edited and expanded. What started off as a fun 'To Do' has turned into some huge saga.

Here's a few things we've included so far:

Get as many selfies with famous people in the background as poss.

Target: At LEAST TWENTY.

Win the jackpot on the 2p machines.

Self-explanatory really. It's a seaside town. Surely there will be amusements. Surely *somebody* has to win on those penny pushers. Right?

<u>Sample chips from every chippie in town.</u>

Rate them out of ten. Chip connoisseurs. We KNOW the best chippie in Greysworth is Abington Plaice; now we're exploring a new town, and a seaside town at that, we must find the finest chips. Saltiness. Tastiness. The best in Skegton.

<u>Learn to love mushy peas.</u>

This is Holly's entry and she refuses to remove it from the list despite the fact that I've told her NO ten thousand times. No way, I'm not on board with that. Way too green and way too gross.

<u>Smash the patriarchy.</u>

This is just on my daily to-do list so it should go without saying but it feels good to tick something you know you'll do anyway. Like, 'getting up'. Or 'brushing teeth'. Zero tolerance for crusty male privilege? Tick.

We take it in turns to play 'Guess What Song I'm Lip-Syncing To' and Holly wins because I can't resist doing Britney every time and as everybody knows it's scientifically impossible to do Britney without the Head Movements. She fist-clenches along to some mystery power ballad as I pull her headphones out.

We are now approaching Skegton-on-Sea. Doors will open on the left hand side. Please ensure you collect all of your baggage before leaving the train.

'We're here!' I jump out of my seat and we frantically shove the evidence of our chocolate feast into the little flappy bin.

We stretch our legs on the platform and take it all in. It feels like we've just walked onto the set of *The Railway Children*. It's so quaint and old-fashioned. The only clue that we're not actually about to run along the tracks with Bobby, Phyllis and Peter is the big orange vending machine and the discarded McDonalds paper bag that catches the wind and glides along in the breeze.

'Breathe! Breathe it in!' Holly inhales dramatically. 'That seaside air!'

I copy her. I close my eyes and let the cold wind batter my cheeks. Picture myself as a Disney mermaid, all scales and shell-boobs, washed up on a big rock and doing the best hair flick of all time.

'*Right. Yes. Yeah. Thirty crates should be arriving later today. We need access to the cafe tent . . .*' A woman speaks into a phone and walks straight towards us.

Holly looks at me for an explanation and I shrug.

Still fully involved with the convo on her phone, this

woman stops before us, flashes a smile and holds out her hand, as if for me to shake.

'Right, OK, many thanks. Do not be late.' She ends the call and grabs my hand. 'I'm Penny. Head of Ops at Skegton Lit Fest. I take it you're Paige and Holly from Bennett's Bookshop in Greysworth?'

She talks without breathing and it throws me. I stumble over my words. 'Yes. Oh hi. Yes, I'm Paige.'

'And I'm Holly. Thanks for having us.'

'Not at all. Thanks for helping out.'

This is when I notice that she has one of those earpiece thingies in her ear. It's attached to a microphone that clips around her neck. Like she's performing at the Brit Awards or something.

'There is so much to do. Follow me, this way; I'll show you to your accommodation.'

So *she's* our Festival Boss.

'She doesn't strike me as someone who'll be up for karaoke with us, Hol,' I whisper.

'Well, that hands-free mic begs to differ! It's official: I'm making it my mission to have a go on that thing before we're back at this station.'

I snort with LOLs and double-step to keep up, lugging my hat box after me.

Acknowledgements

Firstly, I'd just like to acknowledge how weird it is to actually be writing actual acknowledgements. Although the making of *Bookshop Girl* has felt like millions of hours in my pants with my laptop, and thousands of Jaffa Cakes, and hundreds of repeats of Robbie Williams' *Greatest Hits*, there are tonnes of gorgeous people who have helped in making it a Real Thing, with a barcode and pages and acknowledgements.

I'd like to thank my agent, Polly Nolan, for making my I'd-like-to-thank-my-agent dreams a reality. You're one of the coolest people I've ever met. Thank you for looking after me and Paige.

Massive-duty-free-airport-Toblerone-sized thank you to my editor Fliss, and everybody else at Hot Key, for believing in Paige, for making this happen, and plying me with pink Starbursts.

The first ever person I showed this to was Jen Bell – who was pretty busy being a bestselling author, hello – when she told me to go for it. Thanks, babe, I owe you one. A really massive one.

Thank you to my first ever bookshop family. The people I had around me when I was Paige's age (and was tripping over art-school boys rather than starting any kind of high-street revolution). Emma Mileham – you gave me a job when I was sixteen, you made me a Bookshop Girl. Andrew and Grace – you made working in a bookshop so fun back then that I've spent the past decade pretty sure that I don't want any other kind of job ever.

To my hilarious, talented, supportive friends who have read parts of this, and listened to me whinge and cry and blabber on and on and on and on about where this is going – thank you. Spesh thanks to Dave (for slipping into the psyche of a teenage girl so easily) and to Jo and Catrin and Gianni and Clare. Thank you, Neil, for christening Paige Turner.

To my darling best girls, Bree and Cere. I don't know who or where I'd be without you. Thank you for holding my hands when I need a wee on the night bus home. You raise me uuuup so I can stand on mountains. You make everything I do feel glamorous.

Maurice Mariotti, you're so dreamy. I fancy you even more than Paige fancies Blaine Henderson. I love you even more than chips and mayonnaise and the happy bit at the end of *Dirty Dancing*. Thank you forever for being my number one fan.

In the process of writing and sharing this, everybody kept loving the Mum character. 'She's so funny' and 'she's so close to Paige'. I hadn't even meant for that to happen. I hadn't even noticed it happen. Well, not on paper. I always knew that my mum, the woman responsible for choreographing a dance routine to the *Big Brother* theme tune and turning every single interaction with a shop assistant into A Funny Thing That Happened Today, is the best friend I'll ever have. Thank you for the lifetime of material you've provided me and Oscar with. I'd say this is for you, Mum, but you wouldn't want me to do it for you. You'd want me to do it for me.